Ghosts
of the Georgia Coast

Don Farrant

Illustrations by Regina Stahl Briskey

Pineapple Press, Inc.
Sarasota, Florida

To Jean, who is skeptical about ghosts but gave me cheerful assistance and moral support anyway! She helped me along the way.

Inquiries should be addressed to:

Pineapple Press, Inc.
P.O. Box 3889
Sarasota, Florida 34230

www.pineapplepress.com

Library of Congress Cataloging-in-Publication Data
Farrant, Don.
        Ghosts of the Georgia Coast / Don Farrant.—1st ed.
                p.   cm.
            ISBN 978-1-56164-265-6 (pbk. : alk. paper)
Ghosts—Georgia. 2. Haunted places—Georgia. I. Title.

BF1472.U6 F36 2002
133.1'09758—dc21

2002074967

First Edition
10 9 8 7 6 5 4 3 2

Design by Shé Heaton
Printed in the United States of America

Contents

Acknowledgments

I am indebted to these compatriots, who helped so much in the search for material to complete this book. They all displayed patience with a persistent researcher. In Chatham County, Margaret Wayt DeBolt, Sam Morris, and especially Bob and Betty Newell. In Liberty County, Rita Geiger, Joyce Ryan, Ben and Frances Collans, Jason Baker, and Marie Brantley. In McIntosh County, Cornelia Bailey, Lynn Thomas, Ann Davis, Carrie Tirrell, Buddy Sullivan, Jack and Debi d'Antignac, Mike Sellers, Joe Sellers, Bob Monroe, Duane Harris, Lucy Lea, and Marshall Brainard. In Glynn County, George Parmalee, Harry Paisley, George Baker, Heather Heath, Rob Asbell, Judy Asbell, Al Holland, Hal Sieber, John Eckhoff, Karen Jacobs, Mickie Jessup, Susan Whitney, Deborah Clark, Bill Jenkins, and Trish Buie. In Camden County, Richard and Barbara Crisco, Tara Fields, Frank Ward, Terrill Porter, Rodney Sheffield, Darren Harper, Shelia Willis, Patricia Barefoot, Joe Shaffer, Eddie McCullough, Sandy Colhard, and Charles Moss.

I've found that librarians and museum employees are always helpful to a researcher, and I want to especially recognize Darren Harper of the Bryan Lang Library in Woodbine, Georgia, and Martha Conroy at the Darien Library. Also, special thanks to Joann Clark, curator of the Midway Museum in Liberty County.

I am deeply indebted to Hal Sieber of Greensboro, North

Carolina, for much of the information found in Chapter 25. A former Library of Congress writer and editor of the Black Perspective Series, Mr. Sieber is the author of *In This, the Marian Year*, nominated for the National Book Award in 1956, and *The Literary, Political, Medical and Legal Status of Ezra Pound*, published by the Library of Congress in 1958. Mr. Sieber has conducted personal research both in Georgia and in Nigeria, and his knowledge was indispensable in describing the incredible saga of the Igbos.

Foreword

I heard my first ghost story at a Boy Scout campout when I was twelve years old. The counselor told one so scary, so chilling, that he had a bunch of quivering, wide-eyed lads staring at the fire. It was great fun. I hung on every word and loved it.

I've lived in many places but like the South best. We have magnolias, palms, and azaleas, and it's probably true there are more ghosts per acre than a whole lot of other places. The moonlight on the ocean and the shrouds of Spanish moss dangling from the oaks don't do anything to dispel the image.

In the early years of this new century, we find a great and growing interest in the supernatural. Vast, indeed, are the many branches of what is broadly referred to as the occult—astrology, witchcraft, telepathy, clairvoyance, even vampirology. You'll be relieved to know we don't get into these related fields in *Ghosts of the Georgia Coast*. We stay strictly with ghostly matters. Here is a book that covers this fascinating subject with a mixture of information and creepiness, plus smatterings of historical background thrown in.

Talking to people about ghost stories can be fun. When you ask about their experiences, there's one good way to tell if they are on the level. Does their response indicate they have memorized every detail and just can't wait to tell you all about it? If so, that's a great sign. Along with this enthusiasm, a certain "ring of truth" will come across, and then the interviewer can be pretty sure the story is authentic. If that feeling of "I *really* saw this" does not come across or if it's too wild or far-fetched, you might have cause to doubt the story.

Some of these stories were not told to me personally, of course. They came from museums and libraries, from the faded pages of books or newspaper clippings about the Golden Isles of Georgia. The majority, however, came from face-to-face contacts with locals, and I am happy to report that all of the stories related personally to me came from witnesses who had that certain enthusiasm, that ring of truth. This made them fun to be with, and I chose to believe them. I hope you will feel the same way.

Consider, for example, Brewster, resident spook in the old house in McIntosh County. I sat down with one of the homeowners, and we talked for more than an hour about Brewster in the very halls where he dwells! Similarly, I heard firsthand accounts of the mysterious happenings in the old theater from the director of the Golden Isles Arts and Humanities Association, who related her vivid experiences while I recorded her story.

It was Henry W. Longfellow who said, "All houses wherein men have lived and died are haunted houses. Through the open doors the harmless phantoms on their errands glide, with feet that make no sound upon the floors." We can't escape the evidence. Paranormal things are happening. Yes, something is out there! It's my hope that this book will give you an entertaining, perhaps pleasantly chilling appreciation of it all. But, remember, don't read this book late at night!

Introduction

The moon, lighting the forest aisles, penetrates the age-old oaks, their branches draped with Spanish moss. The light filters down past massive trunks and lays a silver mosaic on the ground below. The atmosphere is heavy with nostalgia and the shading of antiquity. There were happenings here—events of local and national importance—and the mystic perception of these past events is ever-present. The ancient lure of the islands wraps itself around you like a blanket.

This is the Georgia coast, land of legend. Here the Creek Indians built their villages and left giant rings in the earth. Here General Oglethorpe spurred his British troops to fight the Spaniards. Here pirates looted, stealing the bells of the Spanish missions to melt them down for artillery and ammunition. Here the English colonists clung precariously to their tiny settlements. Here the blockade runners beached their boats during the Civil War after leading the Yankee blockaders on a desperate chase, only to elude them in the low-lying clouds along the shore.

Walking the woodland paths, treading the smooth sands of the beaches, or sniffing the wafted scents of coastal marshlands is like stepping backwards in time. You can almost hear the shouts of Spanish soldiers and the rattle of their armor as, landing on the beaches, they rush to lay siege to a British fort. You can smell the aroma of their campfires. You can hear the chants of the slaves, toiling in the cotton fields or the war cries of the Creek Indians as they prepare for the warpath.

At the seashore you can almost see countless footprints leading back across the sands of time. The barefoot slave was here; the planter's steady tread; the Indian's moccasin; and the heavy boot of the pirate. On these same beaches there was happiness, tragedy, the wonder of young love, and the violence of cruel murder. It all adds to the special mystique, that certain magic of these storied islands.

There were dark and somber happenings here, gruesome tribal rites and ancient voodoo ceremonies, remembered and practiced by the slaves. A root, for example, planted beneath a doorstep or a mattress could be a powerful hex, perhaps putting a lasting spell of evil on someone's enemy or rival. Do certain spirits, through the years, remember all this? Do they still hearken to the dramas of witchcraft and the tokens of evil? Do the ghosts of today take lessons from the mystic rites of yesterday?

Maybe part of the answer lies in our old ruins. In the Golden Isles they are easy to find: crumbling slave cabins, plantation homes, ancient forts—even a slave hospital that once cared for the five hundred slaves of Retreat Plantation. Every one of these structural ruins has its own aura. When you walk closely around them, as I have on many occasions, you get a sense of vibrant bygone living. You are suddenly closer to the tremors of joy and pain, the triumphs and the agonies of those shadowy figures of long ago.

When automobiles first came to St. Simons Island (the first island to have a causeway connected to the mainland), the roads gave out groans of protest each time a vehicle passed over. Or so the story goes. Where were these unearthly moanings coming from? One woman, a writer and historian, had an answer. Roadbeds on the island, she wrote, were constructed from the Creek Indians' prehistoric mounds; thus the awful sounds were cries of anger from spirits of the natives whose burial places had been disturbed.

In these pages, you'll find lots more evidence that the supernatural is alive in the Golden Isles. The old cemeteries, the moss-draped oaks, the scuttling ghost crabs on the beaches, even the moonlit path that glitters across the water—all seem to be signs of deeper mysteries nearby, mysteries we cannot understand.

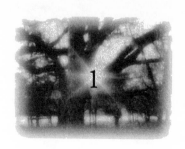

Mary de Wanda
Ghost Girl of the Isles

St. Simons Island

Only the oaks are ancient enough
To remember how, on Gascoigne Bluff,
The news was brought that her lover drowned
In the hungry sea beyond the sound.

Only the oaks can whisper now
Of Mary's grief, or tell you how
She watched the ever-empty sea . . .
And watches still, through eternity.

—Julia Eubanks Evatt

The plane, an Eastern Airlines Martin 303, was making a night approach at Malcolm McKinnon Airport on St. Simons Island. In the mid-1950s, there was no tower, only a flight service station handling radio contact. All was going well as the crowded airliner slanted toward the field, slowing its engines, its landing lights illuminating the way ahead.

Suddenly the co-pilot yelled into his mike: "What's that woman doing on the runway?"

"That's impossible," said a voice from the station. "I don't see anything."

"A woman, I tell you, on a horse—holding a light of some kind."

The heated exchange continued. The co-pilot was sure he was seeing a woman holding a lantern, wearing a long, shroudlike garment, sitting on a horse right in the middle of the runway. Words of disbelief continued to erupt from the control station.

Finally came the instructions: "Don't land . . . don't land! Pull up and go on to Jacksonville."

This was only one of many spectral observations of Mary the Wanderer, or "Mary de Wanda," as it would be in Geechee, the strange lingo created by generations of Africans who had developed a blend of old native words and a smattering of English. And Mary de Wanda would be the name applied to one of the most chilling ghosts ever to roam the Golden Isles.

The mystery of Mary can be traced (legends say) to the hurricane of 1824. A lovely young girl with long, flowing hair was desperately in love with a young man, said to be a son of Raymond Demere, a nineteenth-century planter. The girl, whose name was

Mary, was a ward and house servant to the Demere family, and Raymond Demere sternly disapproved of his son's liaison with her. Deeply in love, the two had been meeting secretly.

One morning the lad quarreled bitterly with his father. Still simmering from the argument, he went to the river landing on St. Simons and shoved off in a small boat, planning to row to the mainland. He had no premonition of the deadly change of weather that would catch him unprepared. By mid-morning, hurricane-force winds were blasting the coastal islands.

All day the hurricane lasted. Meanwhile, Mary had missed her lover. Her search for him brought her to the waterfront, where she remained, wandering the shore for many hours while the storm raged. That night, when there was a lull, she found the capsized boat, half-submerged beneath the waves. Legend has it that she was so distraught with grief she cast herself into the foaming waters.

Is Mary still watching and waiting for her lover's return, especially on stormy nights? From a number of reports, this would seem to be the case. She carries a lantern; sometimes she appears in a long, white garment that looks like a shroud.

Carolyn Butler, a former third-grade teacher at St. Simons Elementary School, saw something she believed to be Mary. Carolyn was in front of her house one day, and a "thing" appeared—not human but more like a big white blob. This was in the neighborhood where Mary had done her wandering, and Carolyn, who had heard the legends, was sure it was a misty, partial appearance of the well-known island spirit. "You just know when you've seen a ghost," Carolyn said later. "You've never been colder in your life, and then you break out in heavy perspiration."

The incident brought shakes and trembles to both Carolyn and her dog, Boots, who ran away from home as a result and camped out at a nearby store. Carolyn coaxed him back several times, but Boots wouldn't stay; in a short time he'd run away again. His fear seemed to stem from the terror of that one experience.

Another sighting, believed to be Mary, was experienced by John Symons, a visitor to the island, sometime around 1940. John and his wife, restless one hot night (before the days of air conditioning) went for a cooling car ride around 2 A.M. They were heading down the long road that parallels the airport runway when suddenly, alongside the road ahead, a strange vision appeared. They both saw a woman, wearing what looked like a long dress with a white veil, standing in front of a horse.

Just at that moment the car windows fogged over with an icy mist—an impossibility on such a warm night. John had to open his door and stick his head out to see anything. As he slowed the car he looked back. For a moment the horse and woman were visible; then, in an instant, they both disappeared. It took the two quite a while to stop shivering from the experience.

Have all sightings of Mary de Wanda been as chilling? Well, not exactly. George Parmelee of St. Simons Island decided a playful prank wouldn't hurt anything. George, a teenager during World War

II, says, "Night activity was pretty well limited during the war. Because of greatly reduced light, during our blackout restrictions we were able to pull a neat trick involving Mary the Wanderer."

George and some friends draped some black silk fishing line over a telephone wire on one side of Beachview Drive, near the St. Simons village. Then they tossed the same line over the wires on the other side. Pulling down the sag in the middle, they were able to attach a garment to it. The result? One of George's Mom's old nightgowns hung right in the middle of the street! They hooked it to the line and weighted it with some sinkers, then hoisted it up high. Standing back in the trees, they stood by, holding one end of the line, and simply waited.

When a car came along, they dropped the nightie down to the street. They found that when they pulled the line and shook it just right, it would look like somebody walking. In the semi-darkness, the trick worked like magic. Several motorists stopped, then continued on—much slower this time—with fearful glances back and with fears we can only imagine.

One young couple saw "Mary" and screeched to a halt. George saw one of them leap out of the car and dash for the telephone company, which was just a short distance down the street. They must have called the authorities, because a short time later George heard police sirens coming across the causeway.

The boys, not too worried, decided to continue the trick. Well, "Mary" sure startled the policemen when she dropped in front of them, then seemed to disappear into the night. The cops turned on their spotlight and searched all along the road, thinking they had hit someone. They looked right and left but never thought to look straight up. Finally they gave up and drove away.

The following Monday an article appeared in the Brunswick News about a mysterious new appearance of Mary de Wanda. George and his pals had a good laugh—but never said a word to anyone about it.

Today, a narrow dirt road cuts through the oaks in a southeasterly direction off Demere Road near Charter Hospital. This is Mary Wan Road—and it may be the only road in the South named after a ghost. At one time it continued for a mile or so, ending near the shopping area near the pier. Now it's only 560 feet long and you won't find it on highway maps. You also won't find a street sign to identify it—that's been gone for years.

Mary Wan Road deadends at the fifth green at the Island Club Golf Course. Some longtime residents feel that if the road itself is lost due to continuing development, then the noted ghost herself may, as they say, "dematerialize" for good.

No, Mary hasn't been witnessed lately. Yet her story remains a part of island lore. Grief-stricken and horribly despondent, she had ended her life with that plunge into the angry waters that had claimed her lover. But had her earthly existence truly ended? She hasn't found her true love yet. There are those who say she is still searching, still wandering with a restlessness that will never stop.

2

The Ghost Wore Spats

South Brunswick

The house was solid, plain-looking, dull white—a two-story structure, built in 1854, well before the War Between the States. The story goes that it was floated in on a barge. Its first location was at the corner of First and Bay Streets; then it was later moved to its present location.

Ron Conrad was only six years old when his family moved into the house in South Brunswick. At first there was no hint of unearthly doings. But it didn't take long before strange things began to happen. Ron and his mother, Miriam, lived on the first floor. They listened in fear and wonder to a myriad of persistent sounds that emanated from the second floor. Mainly, they consisted of thumps and footsteps, sometimes embellished by the sound of a toilet flushing all by itself!

At first they didn't think of their unwanted guest as a ghost.

They just lived with those upstairs noises, got used to them, and called their new "presence" Harvey. When they heard a noise, they'd simply say, "Well, there's Harvey again," or, "Harvey, stop that!"

One night when his mother was out working, Ron was sitting on the couch in the living room, watching TV. The TV was right next to the door to the dining room. Imagine the boy's surprise when suddenly a man stood in the doorway! Ron said later, "I freaked." He bolted out of the house and ran to his neighbors.

But Ron remembers that the man was tall with silver hair and bright, penetrating blue eyes. He wore a pin-stripe suit—gray with white stripes. And, "he had an aura about him—almost silhouetted," says Ron. The strangest thing about him (and something Ron had never seen before) was what he later described as "cloth covers for his shoes." This was Ron's first look at spats, fancy shoe protectors worn by well-dressed gentlemen in the early days.

A search of the house revealed nothing. There was no intruder, and everything was in its proper place. Were they dealing with some sort of earthbound spirit, perhaps that of a former occupant who had died in the house? Ron and Miriam asked around and discovered that several people had passed away there. In fact, Miriam did some digging and obtained pictures of all these people. When they were put in a row ("Almost like a line-up at the police station," says Ron), the boy was able to identify Mr. Anthony Sedgwick, who had died in the house of tuberculosis around 1920. Later, Ron discovered he was distantly related to Sedgwick. "I figured that he was my great-grandfather's brother," he says.

There was a certain measure of relief for Ron and his mother now that they had identified the ghost. However, even knowing who he was didn't ease their minds completely: they still had to get used to his presence and try to get comfortable around him. The noises continued, the footsteps and the toilet flushing being the most prominent. One new feature was a chilly floor, and Ron wondered if the ghost caused it. The floor—even in hot weather—would get icy cold. As time went on and Ron grew into manhood, he saw Mr. Sedgwick only in glimpses. Something would whisk past in the hall, seen through an open doorway when the house's occupants were sitting in the living room.

Ron's younger brother, Norman, had an experience one morning when he was about seven years old. He was in bed, just waking up, when he felt a presence near him. Someone is there, he said to himself, and he didn't want to open his eyes. Finally he looked up. Standing at the side of the bed and looking down at him was Mr. Sedgwick! The ghost soon faded from sight, but the boy was frozen in fear. When he was finally able to move, he told his mother about the experience.

Almost every time there was a sighting of Mr. Sedgwick, something negative would happen a short time later. His appearance was a sort of forecast of coming events, and there might be danger. Was the ghost trying to warn them? Did he see what was coming? After one sighting, Ron almost had auto accident. That's why both Ron and his mother remain sure that he is a protector, not malevolent in any way. "He's watching over us," says Miriam.

One encounter with Mr. Sedgwick involved a guest in the house. Miriam was going through a divorce and wanted company with her in the house. She asked her stepmother, Clara, to come up from Florida and spend a couple of days with her. It seems that while Miriam was bothered by the divorce, her stepmother was edgy about something else: she had heard about the ghost, and she once said, "If I ever saw him I would probably leave the house!" Deciding to comfort each other, the two slept together in one large double bed.

In the middle of the night, Clara woke up to see a man standing at the foot of the bed. She looked at him—that halo effect around his head, that pin-stripe suit, and those probing, bright blue eyes—and was not afraid. In a level voice she asked, "What do you want?"

There was no answer. The ghost turned and pointed to the window. Clara felt strangely beckoned and got out of bed. By the time she reached the foot of the bed, the ghost was gone. But she walked to the window and pulled the curtains back. There, standing just outside and looking in, was Miriam's estranged husband. Once he saw Clara, he turned and made tracks in the other direction. Upon hearing that her soon-to-be-ex-husband was there, Miriam said to Clara, "He just wanted to see if anyone was with me! And when he saw you, he skedaddled."

After this incident, Miriam felt even more strongly that the spirit was acting as a guardian, protecting her from danger. "He seems to be especially protective of women," she said. "But that makes sense. It comes from the era he lived in, when gentlemen were that way." But she can't forget that each time he appears, something will happen. Some danger will threaten and it might cause discomfort, even suffering, to some member of the family.

From time to time, the upstairs of the house was rented out. In one case, not so long ago, the tenant was a young, single, working man. When he brought in a special guest one night, his girlfriend, he didn't realize that a former resident of the house might not approve! While he was entertaining the young lady, he suddenly looked up and saw in the doorway an elderly, well-dressed man staring at the two of them with a sternly disapproving look. The young Romeo was caught in an embarrassing moment, true, but he had no fear; instead he was angry. He took off after the stranger and the ghostly figure ducked out the door. In hot pursuit, the young swain chased him down the hall. The chase ended when the quarry ran *through* a wall. (Ghost researchers explain this in a logical way. Moving spirits always follow a path that traces their original steps during their active lifetime. That's why they can walk through recently placed furniture, for example. When they go through a wall, it's simply a sign that there was originally a doorway at that spot.)

One night, after Mr. Sedgwick had been quiet for a long time,

Miriam saw him—but it was just a fleeting glance as he stalked the hallway. This was late in 1999 and it prompted her to muse: "Now that I've seen him again, I'm wondering if something is going to happen. Will one of my sons be in an accident? Will something happen to the house?"

But in this case, nothing happened. Then, only a short time later, Miriam had another experience with her silent companion. She was in bed with the flu, and when a head poked into the doorway of her bedroom, she knew exactly who it was. In a moment he was gone, but the head reappeared a few moments later. He's checking on me, Miriam thought to herself, and this time she was ready with a comment.

"Anthony," she called out, using his first name. "Don't worry about me. I'm all right."

The head in the doorway disappeared.

Miriam recovered fully from the flu. But she is glad Mr. Anthony Sedgwick is still on guard. She doesn't want him to leave. Having that sort of faithful guardian gives her lots of reassurance.

3

The Phantoms in the Shopping Mall

McIntosh County

The man never made an orthodox appearance. He would simply "appear" just inside the front door of the store in the mall, looking at Louise Benton, who attended the cash register. The man showed up only in late afternoons. He never stayed long. He didn't buy anything. He didn't browse in the store—just stayed in one spot. Nobody ever saw him come in or go out.

A couple of times, Louise turned to the strange visitor and asked, "Can I help you?" The fellow, perhaps thinking his privacy was being threatened, would always dissolve away. Maybe it was just as well, Louise figured, because his head was kind of repulsive. She remembered it with a shudder. His noggin was just sort of "not there"; it was vague, smoky-looking, and seemed to have no solid matter at all. He was dressed in what looked like modern sport clothes—a dark blue, knit, polo-style shirt and beige khaki pants.

The guy had good threads, Louise thought, but each time he appeared he caused her to have the shivers.

Louise, who had a certain measure of psychic awareness, figured she knew what the man at the door represented. He must be an earth-bound spirit, she said to herself. She didn't feel threatened and she made up her mind to go on working, in spite of her nervousness over such a strange presence (which, by the way, no one else could see).

The store was in a huge mall at the site of an old rice plantation in McIntosh County. Louise, who stood at the checkout desk, stayed plenty busy during working hours. Occasionally, she helped out on the floor, pointing customers toward the things they wanted. Sometimes she would make trips to the back room to pick up extra stock. And besides the ghostly man at the front door, there were other manifestations of the paranormal in that retail store.

One day, hearing noises in the back room, Louise went back to investigate. Some items had mysteriously fallen off the shelves. While putting them back (and counting some money that had spilled out of a container), she had her first glimpse of what would be continuing and hard-to-understand contacts with store-dwellers who weren't really there.

Louise was aware of two little shapes scampering around the stockroom. She never saw them directly, only peripherally. Each time she turned to look directly at them, the figures were gone. They were playful little nymphs, dark in color. Louise concluded, after several "sideways visions," they must be two small, black girls playing tag in a frisky manner all around the room. They wore plain, simple-looking dresses. Old-fashioned, small braids covered their heads, and they were barefoot. Louise guessed they could be no more than four or five years old.

Deciding the girls were friendly, Louise got so used to them that she ignored them and didn't mention them to other employees. Every now and then things would fall off the shelves, and the noise was irritating. Louise was the only person who knew what caused the noise, and she was the only one in the store having contact with the two girls.

The next unwanted guests Louise found in the store were two white boys who were seen directly many times. They seemed to be around eleven or twelve years old and were dressed in simple, well-worn, homespun clothes, giving them the appearance of boys who might be on an old wagon train in the movies. Not only were they full of mischief, but one day when one of them appeared near Louise, he turned and grinned at her before he scampered away. His face seemed to say, "Ha, ha, you can't catch me!"

As before, no other employee or customer saw the boys, and Louise, knowing others would not believe her, didn't tell anyone. For a time, things went along peacefully, but soon enough something weird began to happen in just one area of the store.

It was a single section of shelving, not large, and customers not only wouldn't buy the stock here, they wouldn't even stand in front of it. They would always move away rather quickly. Louise, standing there one day herself, had a chilling sensation of what the trouble was. She got an intense feeling that someone or something was right behind her. Turning, she saw no one, but the sensation of another presence was so intense, so frightful, that she moved away. This was a deep mystery in the store and was never explained.

Louise employed Sherry, a teenaged girl, as an assistant. Sherry was a faithful employee and although she never had any experiences with the ghosts, the phantoms must have liked her. When Sherry finally left the job, something happened that convinced Louise that the spirits were upset. There was a tremendous noise of falling objects and all the merchandise in one corner of the store fell off the shelves! Customers asked, "Is it an earthquake?"

Louise knew better. Shaking her head to the customers and smiling, she said to herself, "No, not an earthquake. The 'guests' in the store just didn't want to see Sherry go."

Research shows that the old Sidon Plantation, one of the largest and most prosperous in McIntosh County during the antebellum period, was in the exact spot where the mall now stood. Somewhat west of Darien, it was one of several plantations owned by James Smith. In the decade before the Civil War, a portion of it was acquired by Smith's grandson, Dean Munro Dunwody. The land was originally a Crown Grant in 1757, later made into a rice plantation in 1810. When the mall went in, historians pointed out that the old plantation house had been in the middle of the plot, just about where Louise's store was placed. And the yard, a big one, would have circled around the house, so it covered a lot of ground.

A likely explanation for the presence of the two black girls comes from the notebook of an old country doctor. He was Dr. James Holmes, who lived many years in McIntosh County and wrote a column called "Dr. Bullie's Notes" for the local paper. ("Bullie" was a lifelong nickname, a reference to the doctor's encounter with a bull in his youth.) In one of his journal entries, penned in 1870, he recalled answering a medical emergency at Sidon Plantation during the antebellum period.

> I remember one morning making a professional visit to Sidon, Mr. James Smith's place, because four little Negroes were terribly scalded by the upsetting of a large pot of boiling water near the plantation hospital door. I sent to the house for rags and covered all the scalded or burned surfaces with an ointment made of soot scraped from the kitchen chimney, a spoonful or two of lard and the whites of a few eggs. I rubbed it all together to the consistency of honey, reapplying as it flaked off. There was little or no inhalation of steam and the recovery of the little sufferers was very rapid. This dressing can be made in any household and away from medical assistance.

Could the ghosts of the two little girls be explained by this incident? Could they have been daughters of one of the household servants? Could two of the four mentioned by the doctor have died? This would be contrary to the doctor's words: ". . . the recovery of the little sufferers was very rapid." The real presence of children here, however, seems significant. Conceivably, two of them could have died as children through sickness or a later accident. Such a thing could be a plausible explanation for the sighting of spirits years later.

If only the complete story could be told, perhaps we could even know who the young man at the store's entrance was.

More Ghostly Encounters at the Mall

It was a day like any other at this same shopping mall in McIntosh County. In one ladies' apparel store, the door's alert system kept going off. The store manager looked up each time, expecting to see a customer walk through the door, but she never saw a soul. The woman shrugged it off, thinking there must be a short in the wiring. She turned her attention to a shipment that had just come in that day.

Then the manager heard a noise in the stockroom. She stopped what she was doing, preparing to go take a look. At that moment, a face appeared at the stockroom door! With a gasp, the manager found herself looking at a face with a ghostly glimmer. It moved forward and there was a body attached to it. The image floated toward her, but the manager, frozen in fear, could do nothing but stare.

The image was that of a woman, highlighted with an unearthly glow. She wore a long, white dress and had long black hair that seemed to be blown by the wind as she moved. She headed straight for the front door, then disappeared. At the same time the alert on the door sounded.

That manager, unable to get over her fear, quit her job that very day.

On another occasion, a security guard was patrolling the parking lot after hours, making sure everything was secure and everyone had left safely. He was riding a golf cart behind the stores, near the trash pickup area, when he saw someone who just didn't belong there!

It was a man on a horse, and he certainly looked like a Native American. In silent wonder, the guard stared, expecting that the stranger would do or say something. However, the Indian didn't move at all but merely sat proudly on his mount, looking at the security guard, then dissolving away into nothing. Afterwards, the security guard found that others had seen the Indian, always on his horse, always in the same pose and posing no threat. He seemed to be standing guard, for what reason, no one knows.

A variety of other odd things have happened on the premises. For example, a young woman who worked at a clothing store remembers that mannequins would fall over during the night, setting off the security alarm. For several days, the mannequins would be secure, then for some reason fall over when there was no one in the store.

Do these incidents have anything to do with the fact that the mall was supposedly built on an old Indian burial ground? One former mall employee believes they are caused by Indian spirits that have no desire to cause harm. "It's just as though they want you to know they are there," she says.

4

Strange Happenings in the Old Theater

Brunswick

Joan Stevens is executive director of the Golden Isles Arts and Humanities Association in Brunswick, Georgia. Joan knows there's lot to be done before this group serves the community the way she wants it to. Headquarters for the association is the Ritz Theater, a downtown show-biz landmark since 1890. Someday, says Joan, the Ritz will be a major cultural arts center for the area: "Just think—music, art, dance. Here we could have all of them, providing a great service to the area, and all under one roof."

Among the many changes and improvements needed, renovating the old building has been the biggest problem. True, the Ritz is getting thousands of dollars from sales tax funds, but that money will cover only redesigning the theater, replacing the roof, and bringing the building up to fire code. A lot of needed repairs and alterations in the auditorium itself will have to be put on hold.

The historic Ritz Theater
(by permission of the Golden Isles Arts and Humanities Association, Brunswick, GA)

Joan works doggedly on the Ritz, which used to the Brunswick Opera House but was converted to a movie house in the 1930s. In the process of working there alone, Joan finds, every now and then, that she is not the only one in what she thought was a deserted building.

I never, ever believed in ghosts. That is, until I moved here. I had been raised to believe there were no such things—and whatever my mother and father told me, I believed to be true. But I have seen and heard too many things I cannot explain in logical fashion whatsoever since I have moved to the Golden Isles. Yes, I am convinced—

there are such things as ghosts!

I don't know why there seem to be so many in this particular area. Is it because history is so rich, or the salt marshes and sea air take hold of people and they don't want to leave? Another thing: the ghosts or spirits I've had the unfortunate pleasure to run across seem to be trying to stay connected to something or some place—or some*one*—that ties them to this area.

Joan, whose office is at the Ritz, spends most of her days and many evenings in the old building. One day in the fall of 1998, Joan got a call from a fellow in the technical crew who had been in the building the night before, hanging lights in the stage area, getting ready for an upcoming show. He was apologetic, saying he'd be back during the day to finish up but did not want to be alone in the building late at night ever again.

"Why?"

"Well, there were several strange sounds coming from the side of the theater, kind of a banging on the walls. I didn't think too much about it, but then I heard what sounded like footsteps offstage, coming onto the stage." Continuing, he described a shot of cold air—and then seeing the back curtain move as if someone were passing behind it. He decided at that point it was time to go.

A few weeks later, Joan went up to the storage space on the second floor where there used to be apartments. She was digging around through old gear, and there seemed to be someone behind her. She turned around but there was nothing there. Later, while looking for something else, Joan again felt the presence. She turned but, as before, there was nothing there. When it happened a third time, she laughed to herself and began to talk out loud: "It's the way people talk to themselves when they get scared! Something like 'OK, whoever that is, just leave me alone now.' And then, I swear, I heard footsteps going away from me, down the hall. It sounded like high heels—and no one wears high heels in our office if we can help it. So I eased myself out of there and headed back downstairs to find a crowd!"

A few nights later, Joan was alone in the theater. "I was shutting things down for the night and had to cross the stage to where the dimmer is for the house lights. And when I hit center stage, I heard footsteps from offstage coming this way, and then saw the curtain move, disturbed by something behind it." Joan called out, "Hello, hello!" but no one answered. Then she saw the figure of a woman crossing the stage. "She came towards me and reached out her hand. She touched my face."

The figure was elderly, somewhat wrinkled, plainly dressed, and stooped over. Joan was not so much frightened as overcome with remorse and sympathy, because the woman had a look of intense sadness.

"I'm so sorry," said Joan, and the woman walked away.

A few days later, two women came into the Ritz. One of them was perhaps middle-aged, but her companion was much older. Joan looked at them, wondering what they wanted, and the older woman sat down and began to talk.

She asked for "Kate."

At first there was no explanation, but in the course of the conversation, Joan learned that her daughter, who used to live in an upstairs apartment, had killed herself on the premises. And her name was Kate. Just when it happened, or by what means, no one knows—but this same story was apparently well known. It had been whispered around the theater, without any further details, by more than one person.

Joan describes Kate's mother as short and stooped, although quite well-dressed. According to Joan, she "looked like she didn't get out into the world very much, and perhaps needed someone to take care of her.

Could there be a tie-in here? Could the spirit on the stage be Kate? It seems likely because the ghost, although looking careworn and tired, appeared to be late middle-aged, and that's about the age Kate was at the time of the tragedy. This end of the drama remains a mystery.

Other ghostly happenings have been reported in the old theater, especially noises. Stage workers and others have heard many, especially at night. For the most part, the sounds come from the side of the auditorium where stairs lead to the old apartments. Joan says, "It's dark up there and there's no electricity. It's scary, especially when it's raining or stormy. I try not to go up there any more than I have to." Laughing, Joan likes to remind people that the theaters of the world have always attracted ghosts. "Some of them, I'll bet, are old actors and they are still hams!" she says.

Whether or not the Ritz Theater has ghosts, it surely does have an interesting history. Built at the turn of the twentieth century, the Grand Opera House was a distinctive landmark in the city of Brunswick. It was described by the *Brunswick News* in 1907 as "one of the prettiest and most thoroughly arranged playhouses in the South." The opera house featured musical performances, and the playhouse also went through the vaudeville era in the 1920s. Many of that era's star performers appeared on its stage. It was renamed the Ritz Theater in the 1930s when it was converted to a movie house.

Thousands knew and loved the theater during its motion picture days, when it featured the finest products of Hollywood. Its shining hour came in 1956, when portions of the movie *The View from Pompey's Head* were filmed in Brunswick, chiefly in and around the old Oglethorpe Hotel. The world premier of the movie was screened at the Ritz, and Richard Egan, who had starred in the picture, attended. While in town, he stayed at the Oglethorpe, which was just kitty-corner from the theater.

But, alas, along came hard times. The Ritz closed its doors on December 2, 1976, a victim of falling revenues, competition from newer theaters, and changing times. The city of Brunswick bought the old playhouse in 1980. Renovations began. During this time, the Ritz hosted certain events, such as the Miss Golden Isles

Pageant, but it could never be called a moneymaker for the city.

In 1990 the Golden Isles Arts and Humanities Association took over management of the theater. The association wanted to promote performing arts of all types. The association looked at the two upstairs floors, hoping to make them into offices or studios for artists. Before they were used as apartments in the 1960s, these rooms had once housed the offices of a railroad company.

In 1992 the theater was experiencing growing pains and had been operating at a loss. Even so, it had hosted more than one hundred events during the previous two years and had been fully restored to its turn-of-the-century appearance. Larry Evans, local architect and arts group member, says, "We can't say the theater will ever make money." But, he concludes, the place, even while operating at a loss, will always have value to the city as well as tremendous cultural value.

The hopes and dreams for the future of the Ritz began coming true with a big bang on September 20, 2001. All of Brunswick was agog with a special party, Puttin' on the Ritz, celebrating the gala reopening of the old theater. The future is bright for the Ritz, which will feature performances of music, drama, movies, and other arts.

5

Brewster:
A Friendly Presence

Crescent

t was at Crescent, on the island-studded coast of Georgia near Darien, that a bizarre, mysterious tale of spirit doings unfolded. The ghost involved was no malevolent presence, though, but a friendly protector of the family.

Back in the 1940s, members of the d'Antignac family owned a house in McIntosh County that dates from the administration of George Washington. The present owners, Jack and Debi d'Antignac, are in the shrimping business. Francis Brewster seems to live there, too, and it doesn't worry Jack and Debi at all.

Having researched the history of their abode and talked to Jack's parents about it, Jack and Debi concluded that Francis Augustus Brewster had lived there for a while. Formerly of Hampden, Connecticut, he had been a physician and clergyman and was an eighth-generation descendant of the elder William

Brewster of the Plymouth Colony. In 1898 he moved to Crescent to be with his son and daughter-in-law, who were living in the d'Antignac house at the time. In 1906, he passed away in the house at the age of eighty-nine. Even though Francis Brewster expired there, his spirit, it seems, is still vigilant.

Around 1940, Auvergne d'Antignac, Jack's mother, had an unforgettable encounter with Brewster during the time she occupied the house. "I was sleeping in a downstairs bedroom when I was awakened in the early hours of the morning by a tapping on my shoulder. Sleepily, I looked up into the face of a tall man with blond hair. He said in a low, gentle voice that someone was ill in the back room. We had a number of guests that night, and as I was only half-awake, I thought this person to be one of their friends I hadn't noticed. I allowed him to lead me by the hand down the hall into the dining room."

At this point, amazing things happened. She snapped wide awake and realized that no one in the house fit this stranger's description. He was wearing odd, out-of-date clothes and a high collar that made him look like a pilgrim of antiquity. Still leading her, he walked into the dining room and *through,* not around, a big table. There was no way to follow this ghostly maneuver, and she bumped into the table edge with bruising force. At that point she screamed and ran back to her husband in the bedroom. Auvergne blurted out to her husband that she had "met Brewster—but not formally"!

The two searched the dining room, but by now her strange

escort had disappeared. After her husband had calmed her down, Auvergne returned to her bed downstairs. Imagine her surprise when she found something on her pillow, something deadly. It was a black widow spider!

Had the apparition known about the spider and simply devised the story about a sick person to get her away from her bed?

The most eerie sighting of their household guest took place when Jack d'Antignac's father and uncle saw Brewster in broad daylight while they were sitting on the front porch. As they talked, a man approached, walking from the direction of the nearby marsh. He was tall, with what appeared to be blond or silvery hair, and he wore a high, old-fashioned collar and a long, dark, preacher-style coat. He seemed as solid as anybody else, but the brothers noticed, as he drew near, that a part of him just wasn't there. His legs below the knees were not visible. The figure came up the front steps, entered the house, and climbed the stairs. He was probably heading for what was believed to be Brewster's Room, an upstairs bedroom from which noises occasionally erupted, such as footsteps and the sounds of furniture being moved around. The two men, speechless and quite shaken, didn't tell anybody about this encounter for a long time.

Debi d'Antignac has had plenty of evidence, in the form of footsteps, thumps, and rattles, that Brewster is around. Brewster has also been known to squeeze people's toes when they are reading in bed, but he stops when the lights are turned off. Sometimes there is the sound of a toilet flushing—all by itself. But Debi has seen him only once in the years she has lived in her house. One day she saw a portion of the ghost as he passed through a door she knew was locked. At times she will catch a glimpse of a shadow going past out of the corner of her eye; at other times a deep chill will envelop her.

Then there's the fancy wax candle. It's hard to explain why Brewster didn't want it to stay downstairs. Debi had placed the rabbit-shaped candle on the downstairs hearth. Strangely, she found it the next day on an upstairs table. She knew that neither she nor Jack had moved it. Puzzled, she replaced it on the hearth. But each time she left it on the hearth, it would somehow make its way to the upstairs table the next day. Finally, Debi gave up. "Well, I guess he just doesn't want it downstairs," she said. "And I don't want it upstairs." She gave the candle away.

On one occasion the house's ancient wiring shorted out in a roof section, almost causing a fire. A fire inspector later related that the dry wood next to the frayed wiring had started to burn but that something had put it out. "I can't understand it," he said. "This sort of electrical failure in your house, with such old, tinder-dry beams, would be sure to cause a bad fire. And yet something stopped it before it could spread."

In recent years, Brewster has been pretty quiet. He lives in harmony with Debi, Jack, and daughter Beth. They all feel safe, even comfortable, knowing that Brewster is a dedicated and benevolent guardian of the family.

6

An Old St. Simons
Ghost Story

St. Simons Island

Purple shadows were lengthening on the western edge of St. Simons Island. A calm, all's-well motion swept the tops of palms, magnolias, and oleander as a light evening breeze enveloped the landscape in a feathery touch.

Near the river, separated from the rolling sea by an island-wide stretch of woodlands, stood the ancient settlement of Frederica. The town, founded by Gen. James Oglethorpe, was bravely holding out against the elements, although in this year of 1880 it was over 140 years old. Her fort, mostly in ruins, still assumed an attitude of protection, but neither fort nor town could hide crumbling tabby walls and sagging roofs. Little was left of the original buildings, and in some cases there was nothing but foundation stones, mostly lost under creeping earth and weeds.

One evening, a rowdy gang was engaged in a dice game and tippling at the shack that served as their headquarters. Their frivolity included wine, and a bit too much at that. The hour was late when these young bucks decided the only way to end the evening would be a monumental prank. "Let's see, now. Who'll be the butt of our mischief?"

Finally they decided. The target for their jibes and tricks would be a colleague, one Thad Houser, a quiet, pitiful sort of fellow, poorly clad and more inclined to stay on the sidelines than lead in the forefront of things. Knowing this, the gang decided to "do him in" with a ghostly scheme, one that would provide amusing conversation for weeks to come.

The old British Colonial Graveyard gave them just the setting they needed. Dating from the 1700s, this ancient burial ground was close at hand. The ancient, above ground burial vaults remained, and by looking inside you could see bones, lots of them, completely bare of flesh and exhibiting only a semblance of rottenness that used to be clothing.

The old graveyard was an eerie, disturbing place even in daylight, and after dark was conducive to the most terrifying shakes and shivers. And it was dark—very much so—when gang members hatched their plan.

"Here's the idea," said one of the ringleaders. "We'll buy Thad a brand new hat if he will go to the old bone yard and bring back *one* bone. Later, we might exhibit it around town but he has to get it himself, nobody can help him, and he has to get it tonight." Then one cruel footnote to the scheme was suggested, and it brought smiles and guffaws from the group.

The plan was explained to the intended victim, and Thad found himself torn between his fear of the horrifying place and his yearning for a new hat, for, after all, his old chapeau was decrepit and full of holes. Finally, his desire for sartorial elegance dispelled all doubts. Accordingly, he set out for the chosen spot, not knowing that one of the gang had preceded him, secreting himself *inside* one of the vaults.

In due time, Thad arrived at the burial ground and, finding a vault with a caved-in stone cover, reached down to pick up a bone. He had it! Then he turned, intent on leaving the hideous place as quickly as possible.

Imagine Thad's horror when he heard, in a sepulchral tone, "Put that down. It belongs to me!"

It was a cataclysmic moment. The unsuspecting victim, shocked beyond description, made his exit at record-breaking speed but somehow, in all his panic, clung to his gruesome trophy. He raced back through the shadows to the house where the conspirators were assembled, looking back once or twice to see if—saints preserve us! —a ghastly figure was following him. Somehow he outdistanced the phantom, still grasping the old, Colonial leg bone. The boys were all smiles, anticipating a good laugh at Thad's expense. They heard him say, "Take the bone quick, for God's sake. The owner's after me!"

At this point, Thad fell senseless on the doorstep. Nor could they revive him, and the boys, now full of shame at what they had done, bore him to a couch. Through all that night he failed to regain consciousness, so the next morning the guilt-ridden gang called a doctor.

During the next few days, other physicians were summoned. The medical men feared for Thad's life, so great had been the shock to his system in the terrible ordeal. Finally, thanks to faithful care, the victim came back to the ranks of the conscious. He'd be all right, said the doctors, but would need a lengthy period of recovery.

And, yes, poor Thad got his new hat. This expense, however, wasn't all the boys incurred, for they ended up paying over a hundred dollars in doctors' bills.

7

A Place Where "Ha'nts" Hover

All along the coast

The aura of mystery and adventure that permeates the Georgia
sea islands comes from more than the mossy oaks, the sway-
ing palms, and the dramatic touches of moonlight and soft sea
breezes. This evasive influence, aiding and abetting the whispers of
the occult on our shores, stems directly from the 1700s, when the
first Africans were brought here to work the plantations.

Long before the War Between the States, the scene was set for
phantom doings. Slaves, bringing accounts of ha'nts from Africa,
talked often of visitations by ghosts. "Just superstitions," said the
plantation owners, but were they? Who is to say where reality and
legend overlap?

If someone passed away in a house, it was said, you must not
remove the body until a preacher said a few words; otherwise, a ha'nt
was sure to hover, perhaps for years. You could protect your dwelling

from ghosts by laying a broomstick across the doorway at twilight—no ghost would come during the night. Or dab blue paint all around the doorway. A little salt sprinkled around was also effective; spirits did not like salt.

For some, a paranormal attribute was a vested thing, said the slaves. A baby born with a caul, or membrane, over his face, would have special powers and be able to see ghosts. Or he might have dominion over inanimate things or be able to cast spells.

The ability to conjure was deep magic. A conjurer specialized in putting mystic spells on others. A conjurer could lay a powerful hex on someone by planting an object under that person's doorstep or mattress. The object might be a root or perhaps a bag of strange and gruesome things: a chicken's head, a lizard's leg bone, blood, or graveyard dirt.

In Harris Neck, a little settlement near Riceboro, just down the coast from Savannah, Liza Basden, a well-known resident, was interviewed by a team of researchers back in the 1930s, when she was eighty years old. The researchers were looking for memories of the slavery years—old tales and beliefs that had been handed down, in hushed tones, from one generation to the next.

Liza said she was born with a caul and could see ghosts. Three of her children were born with cauls as well. Liza would see human forms and described them as being just like anybody else, except that some had no heads. She watched them pass back and forth along her walkway. "Maybe they were guarding something buried in the yard," she said.

A man in Yamacraw, another small coastal community, told the same researchers that he saw ghosts every now and then. He remembered that they came in all kinds of shapes— some had no head, some had no feet—just floating by. He said that if you didn't meddle in their business, they wouldn't meddle in yours.

In another interview, Evans Brown, registered pride in his belief in the supernatural and in his unusual ability to see and visualize almost magical things. As a school custodian, he recalled the times, on cold winter mornings, when he would go early to school to make fires. He would hear doors opening and shutting, and sometimes he would *see* the ghost that did it, although he gave no description of the ghost.

With a chuckle, Brown added that local police arrested a man once near the school. They had him by the pants and were taking him to the call box to ring for the wagon. When the police got through talking and turned to look, they found they were holding an old gray mule—and the prisoner had disappeared!

In these sessions with researchers, not all interviewees told of the serious side of ha'nt doings. Some added touches of humor (albeit slightly gruesome humor). For example, Chloe West, a woman of uncertain age, remembered her courting days. When Chloe was young and "receiving company," two men would come to see her. She liked one man better, and the other man was jealous. When the jealous one died, she kept seeing a shadow—that looked just like him come up to her door and disappear. One night he said in a loud voice, "Is that other man still comin' 'round here?" She was scared stiff.

One elderly gentleman who claimed he was eighty-eight told an almost unbelievable story to the interviewers. A fellow from Liberty County came to the plantation selling wings, telling people that they'd be able to fly back to Africa! He would take an order for a pair of wings, measure the customer, and tell him the cost was twenty-five dollars. He asked for a down payment of five dollars. He took many orders for wings, then went away. But the wings never materialized—and the fellow never came back.

This bizarre story comes from the keen memory of a resident of White Bluff on the northern Georgia coast. The man had heard that long ago it was customary for groups of men to go to Blackbeard Island to search for a location to bury their money. Afterwards, one in the group would be selected to be put to death by the others. The survivors were sure that his spirit would stand guard and protect the treasure.

Several of the interviewees warmed up to the subject of ghosts by talking of hags. A hag was a witchlike woman who would pounce on you while you were sleeping. She would press on you with unrelenting force, making you feel as if you were being suffocated.

Superstitions and strong beliefs in the supernatural are more understandable when one remembers that voodoo was brought across the sea with the slave cargoes. Voodoo! A word of rolling mystery, somehow beckoning the nocturnal sound of drums from the

The hag flies by night

depths of the forest primeval. It's a word that brings a shudder, reminding the outsider of the abominations he has read about. Isn't it the symbol of sorcery, depravity and terror?

Well, not exactly. Haitian scholar Jean Price-Mars says voodoo is a religion, not a violent sort of "cult event." He explains: "It results in a deep psycho-nervous disturbance, bordering on paranoia." At gatherings, participants often fall into a sort of violent dance or frenzy.

But voodoo *is* of West African origin, and the practice was carefully nourished and preserved by the slaves. So it was that in ante-bellum days slaves would hold ceremonies—usually late at night and in deepest secrecy. For the most part, plantation owners never knew about these voodoo gatherings, but when the owners did hear about them, it was not surprising that they banned these gatherings, knowing that participation inflamed the imagination.

Today the old habits and practices are gone from Georgia's coast, or nearly so. But does that haze of memory, that veil of occult mysticism, still cast its influence over the sea islands?

Note: Much of the material in this chapter came from *Drums and Shadows, Survival Studies Among the Georgia Coastal Negroes*, Brown Thrasher Books, University of Georgia Press (1940, 1986).

8

The Phantom
in the Lighthouse

St. Simons Island

A cruel murder. Footsteps in the tower. Sightings of a shadowy
form. Tucked away in the lore of St. Simons is the tale of the
ghost in the lighthouse.

Is he still there? Many wonder. Did he ever really climb the
stairs with spectral tread? Or did the wind, the oaks, and the deserted marshlands combine to stir the imaginations of lonely keepers
and their families in days gone by?

It was Sunday morning, February 29, 1880, just eight years
after completion of the new lighthouse and keeper's cottage, which
replaced the old beacon blown up in the Civil War. Serious argu-
ments had caused hard feelings between keeper Fred Osborne and
his assistant, and the two had "stepped outside" to settle it. After bitter words, Osborne threatened his assistant with a pistol, whereupon
the assistant re-entered the cottage, grabbed his shotgun, which was

The St. Simons Lighthouse
(photo courtesy of the Coastal Georgia Historical Society)

loaded with buckshot, and shot Osborne at a range of ninety-eight feet. The pellets hit him in four places, but only one wound was serious, entering his abdomen.

Remorse must have enveloped the assistant right away. He sent for the island doctor, then went to Brunswick and gave himself up.

Later, when released on bond, he performed double watch duty, serving both his shift and that of his stricken boss. Osborne died about a week later.

A new keeper, George Ashball, was appointed the following May. The light at that time (long before electricity and automation) was a kerosene lamp, and its rotation was governed by weights and pulleys. It required rather frequent attention to keep things moving. A short while after this, strange things began to happen. Apparently the attendants weren't the only ones climbing the winding iron staircase!

After the murder, several keepers reported hearing footsteps ascending and descending the tower. The wife of one keeper, thinking she heard her husband coming down from the light chamber, would put dinner on the table for him. But the steps would stop, and she'd blame the ghost for a cold dinner. At other times, the keeper, high in the tower, would hear someone approaching and would later tell his wife, "I thought you were coming up to visit me tonight, but when I looked there was no one there at all!"

Oddly, the footsteps never went above the highest landing at the top of the 129-step stairway or below the lowest landing. Also, the phantom seemed to worry about bad weather, for his steps would be especially loud during storms. If the spirit was indeed old Fred Osborne, could it be that he was standing by at such occasions to make sure the light was working properly?

Dogs owned by the keepers' families were particularly bothered by the footsteps on the stairs and would whine and press close to family members at spook-walking times. Children, on the other hand, got so used to the sounds that they hardly noticed them—but not always. One night a small boy in the cottage got mad because he couldn't sleep. Hearing a crash from his room, his mother investigated and found the lad was so annoyed by the pesky ghost that he threw his shoe at him!

Lighthouse personnel who heard the "spirit steps" generally accepted their spooky guest as harmless. Carl Svendson was keeper from 1907 to 1935, and his family lived in the keeper's cottage. After a time, the Svendsons got so accustomed to the *thump-thump* of the spirit that they accepted what they considered a friendly ghost as part of the family. Not so, however, with one keeper. This man not only heard the thing climbing the stairs but claimed he saw a shadowy form moving around on the grounds, too. From that day on, he refused to stand a watch alone at night and had to be replaced by an assistant who was not afraid of the "unseen."

Today it's hard to believe a grisly crime was committed in this white tower, followed by a paranormal stair-climber, perhaps the earthbound spirit of the murdered keeper. Could the ghost still be hanging around? Perhaps not. Members of the local historical society, who watch over the lighthouse and welcome its many visitors, will tell you that the ghost hasn't been seen, or *heard,* lately. No matter—the story of Fred Osborne remains one of the fascinating stories of old St. Simons.

9

Orange Hall
A Haunted Mansion

St. Marys

S t. Marys, a coastal town near the Florida border, has been
called one of Georgia's best-kept secrets, a place rich in history, natural beauty, and Southern hospitality. Walking through the
riverfront area on a quiet, clear night, you can't miss the magical
glow when moonbeams turn the Spanish moss to silver. The breeze
caresses your cheek, and it's easy to imagine that mere mortals aren't
the only ones doing their thing in this place, a town that dates back
to the mid-1500s.

With all those ancient oaks—some of record size—and all the
picturesque, nineteenth-century homes, you might suspect there are
supernatural presences here. And you'd be right. One mansion located on the main thoroughfare, Osborne Street, stands out from the
others. This is Orange Hall, a landmark structure with an eventful
past. Visit Orange Hall and you'll find a few more "residents" than

Orange Hall (courtesy of Debbie Britt, photographer)

those on the welcoming committee!

As you enter the house, you'll get a cheery welcome from the hostesses and guides. As you venture into the rest of the house, you may feel a different sort of welcome—a feeling of mystery from sources that aren't so much unfriendly as oddly curious and inquisitive. You're sensing the spirits of Orange Hall, and guides will tell you that they are, for the most part, past residents who refuse to leave.

It was around 1825 that a man named John Woods ordered construction of a fabulous mansion on the north end of lot 43 in St. Marys. The builder was his son-in-law, Horace Pratt. The house is a classic example of Greek Revival architecture and has been called "one of the showplaces of the town." It went through a number of owners but always remained a center of social activity. In 1973 it was placed on the National Register of Historic Places.

Tara Fields, well-known historian of Camden County, has done research on Orange Hall and has singled out three different entities who still abide there. One of them, a young girl, is said to be the daughter of the builder, Horace Pratt, who, by the way, was also the first pastor of the storied Presbyterian Church just across the street. Not long after the family moved out of the home, Jane Pratt became ill and passed away.

So it was that little Jane Pratt was living elsewhere, far from Camden County, at the time of her exit from mortal spheres. Somehow she returned, however, and has been glimpsed at night playing with a doll in her bedroom. People will find evidence of her presence the next morning: She leaves the bed rumpled and moves the doll from one place to another.

Tara Fields names two other spectral entities. One is the spirit of an elderly gentleman, who is seen occasionally. The other is a woman always dressed in purple. Supposedly she is seen in photos taken of the front of the building.

An interesting report from one inquisitive researcher who specializes in hauntings suggests that there may be a fourth spirit associated with the mansion. This man relates seeing the apparition of a slender, young man with red hair wearing a uniform of some sort. Although the image was somewhat indistinct, the researcher was certain the uniform dated from a period prior to the Civil War. It could have been French or perhaps American, stemming from the Mexican War.

Standing a few yards from the soldier, the ghost hunter said the soldier seemed to be floating above the floor and didn't have the lower parts of his legs. He stood in front of one of the fireplaces and was apparently staring at something on the mantel. As the inquisitive visitor got closer, the soldier became almost transparent and objects behind him became faintly visible. But nothing changed his stance; he remained motionless in front of the fireplace.

On another occasion, a visitor got permission to videotape the interior of Orange Hall. In one room she found a large mirror on the wall opposite the door. While she didn't notice it while filming, something strange appeared on the film when she reviewed the video. When the camera was panned across the mirror, it picked up the reflection of a faded, somewhat-transparent old man standing in the doorway. The stately old gent is described as having nineteenth century–style clothing, complete with pocket watch and chain, and an angry, disturbed look on his face. Those viewing the video said they could see the old fellow "as clear as day." Was he the spectral image of a long-ago occupant of Orange Hall who just plain didn't appreciate visitors snooping and taking pictures in his bedroom? It's probable he is the same elderly gentleman mentioned by Tara Fields.

There is something uncanny involving one fireplace in the house. Sometimes when someone takes a picture of it, all that comes out is a cloudy, mystic shroud. Yet pictures taken from the same roll of film in other parts of the house will come out all right. Why wouldn't the camera portray the fireplace? Some will refute this testimony. For example, Tara Fields took several pictures of that same fireplace and they all came out perfectly. Tara remarks, "Maybe this particular 'haunt' is fussy about whom he tricks. But, more likely, many [people] just don't know how to take a picture of a black fireplace in a sunlit room with white walls. It's easy to get improperly exposed photos that don't show the fireplace clearly."

People who have checked into the mysteries of Orange Hall all seem to agree that the atmosphere has everything needed for chills and hauntings. Spirit researchers say there is a lot of energy lingering in the halls and the many rooms. You would be correct if you concluded that the storied old mansion is both a historic place and a site of supernatural doings.

10

The Ghostly Battle in the Graveyard

Midway

When the two young fellows visited the Midway Museum in Midway, Georgia, they had something on their minds.

"We've always wanted to do it! We want to go into the graveyard at night, just to see if it's scary."

"Well, if that's what you want to do. . . ." said Mrs. J.C., the curator. She didn't see how two curious boys could do any harm. She told them where the gate was and gave them permission to make their ghostly tour.

That night the lads went into the dark and somber burial grounds. Wide-eyed and trembling, they dodged around the headstones and tried to avoid tripping over the roots of the giant oak trees. Far over their heads came the cry of a night bird, while somewhere in the distance they could hear the hoot of an owl. Embellishing this nocturnal symphony, the rustle and *whoosh* of the wind added a ghostly accompaniment to the atmosphere.

Their exploration was only about half done when they figured they'd had enough and turned to leave. Just at that moment there came a scuffling noise from the back of the graveyard. They strained their eyes to see in the dim light. They could make out the figures of two men, clasped in what seemed to be a bitter fight. They watched in fascination while the men staggered and cursed as they struggled around the grave markers.

The fight looked real, but the boys wondered if the men were really there. All they could make out were the outlines of human forms, vague shapes that looked like men and wore hats but weren't distinct or "full" enough to get a clear view. The boys edged closer. Scared but curious, they continued to watch the fight. Suddenly one of the combatants turned and faced the boys. He extended an arm and pointed right at them, at the same time starting to move toward them in a menacing way!

The boys broke all speed records getting out of there.

A few years later, the two, now young men, made another visit to the Midway Museum. They related the whole story to the curator, and, of course, she was greatly intrigued. Putting together the location in the graveyard where the ghostly fight happened, along with other tales that "tied in," Mrs. J.C. pieced it all together. She was sure the scene was an aftermath of an old story of two lovers, Sylvia and Anthony, and their romance, truly a Romeo-and-Juliet tragedy of forbidden love.

Sylvia came from a good family in the Midway area. Her parents had been encouraging her to get married. When finally the day came that she told them she was in love with a young man and wanted to marry him, they were elated. Little did they know that Sylvia, feeling sure her folks would not approve of Anthony, who was of a different race, had been meeting him secretly in the old Midway burial ground! It was the most private place around, and no one would ever know about their nightly rendezvous. . . .

Sure enough, when her parents finally met Anthony, they disapproved and said she was too good for him. "His station in life is far below yours," they told her. Sylvia's father, a strict, demanding man, actually picked another townsman for his daughter to marry to get her mind off Anthony! She refused, so her father locked her in her room.

That night, knowing Anthony was waiting for her in the graveyard, Sylvia climbed out of her window and ran to meet him. Her search among the oaken trunks and headstones at first revealed nothing, but then she found Anthony. His dead body was hanging from a tree.

Sobbing in grief, she loosened the rope that secured him, letting his body down to the ground. Then she saw it—a knife was buried in his chest. According to one account, there was a note attached to the knife. Picking it up, she saw that it was from her father, and it read: "I told you to stay away from this [expletive]. If you are not going to obey me, I will make you obey."

She screamed, bowing her head over her lover's prostrate body and sobbing in the stillness of the night. Her grief was such that she grasped the knife and killed herself. The next day, a caretaker found the two of them, lying together in the cemetery. For years afterwards, citizens of Midway would say that in late evening you could see the two of them together under one of the giant oaks.

The story of the lovers, perhaps partly based on legend and hearsay, leads directly to an explanation of the battling figures seen by the two boys. The savage fight scene was a ghostly rerun of something that happened there at an earlier date, when the girl's father caught up with Anthony. The tense, desperate struggle between the two had created a psychic disturbance, an energy pattern that would repeat itself many times in the future.

The Crack in the Wall

The desperate struggle and its awful aftermath in the ancient Midway burial ground brought memories of another bloody deed that took place years earlier. Back, far back, when the stone wall was first being built, something happened that led to the legend of the "crack in the wall." A jagged, very pronounced crack at the northeast corner of the brick wall of the cemetery was not made by human hands, people say. It's the ghostly manifestation of an act of violence many years ago.

The wall was built by slaves. One day, two of them quarreled. Their overseer noted that the pair had not finished their work and, as punishment, ordered them to work overtime. That night one of the men killed the other with a brick. The murderer buried his victim under the foundation of the wall. He carefully replaced the brickwork, hoping no one would discover his crime. He then told his master that his companion had run away.

Shortly afterward, a large crack appeared in the wall at the scene of the murder. It was mended, only to crack again. This happened again and again. Years later, the bones of the dead slave were found, but the brickwork kept rupturing, as if the spirit of the victim could not rest. Descendants of slaves would say, "Ain't no use to mend it. It's gonna crack as fast as it gets fixed."

11

Tales of the
Midway Burial Ground

Midway

I t was in Midway, once a Colonial town settled in the 1700s in Liberty County, that so much history took place and so much heritage was born. Here the centuries-old oaks stand guard, the venerable Midway Church still welcomes the faithful, and there's an aura of ever-present nostalgia, along with the mystic wonder of a storied past.

Just across from the church lies the ancient burial ground, still encircled by its weathered stone fence. It was here that the sad tale of a young doctor caught in a love triangle brought on a crisis.

After his wife died, Dr. John Porter acquired not one new sweetheart, but two! His outgoing and romantic nature, combined with the fact that he was lonely, caused him to get involved with two local ladies. Apparently they both loved him as well. His double involvement deepened and became a real problem. Being torn between his two loves, his desperation grew and he often wandered in confusion. How, he asked himself, can I get out of this predicament?

At first, the affair was hush-hush, but it soon ballooned into a real scandal. The shocking truth was soon told and retold all around town: both of the doctor's ladies were in a family way. The doctor was treated as a social outcast. The attitude of the townspeople so bothered the conscience-stricken doctor that he killed himself.

The tragic tale also has a sad aftermath. Dr. Porter's body was laid to rest just outside the stone fence of the cemetery. Not long after, the graveyard was expanded. When the wall was moved out, his grave, along with a few others, was included in the burial ground, which brought a storm of protest. The doctor does not deserve to be buried here, people whispered, since proper Christian interments do not include suicides.

Public disapproval continued, but for a while nothing was done about it. Then supernatural forces seemed to sense the problem— and took matters in hand. After a while, powerful roots from a huge tree began to rise up through the ground and dislodge the coffin. Many wondered, Was someone—or some*thing*—trying to oust the doctor from his resting place?

When a mother and her young son visited the museum just across the road from the old burial ground only a few years ago, they brought with them a question. "We have just visited the burial grounds," said the mother. "Let me ask you, Who placed the beautiful blue floral bouquet, tied with a blue ribbon, on that headstone near the back wall?" The curator could not answer, except to say that

no one from the museum had left it there. Most astonishing of all, however, was the mother's inquiry about something that lay beside the flowers. It was a letter, she said, a letter on old parchment, not paper, written in old-style loving words, such as "Oh, my dearest, why did you do it? Why did you leave me? I could have accepted the other woman, but why, oh, why, did you have to go?"

The curator just listened, dumbfounded. Later, when she went across the street to check on this story, there were no flowers and no parchment letter. Only a bright blue ribbon remained. It seems that although John Porter is only a memory and people have forgotten the love affairs and the scandal, there are signs that his two sweethearts have not forgotten—or at least one of them!

The deadly yellow fever epidemic of 1854 carried many citizens to the Great Beyond. Included in the list of victims were over thirty children, laid to rest in the Midway graveyard.

Jim Dunbar had heard the tales. At midnight on a clear night, it was said, things would happen, especially if there was a full moon. Having heard the stories repeated, Jim was greatly intrigued by one unbelievable thing folks would say: "The ghosts of little children are there. They will play hide and seek with you."

Being adventurous, Jim was adamant to check this out. Why not do a "midnight watch," he said to himself, to see if the little supernatural scamps will play with me. On his first trip alone into the graveyard, he had no fear, even though he could sense other presences around him. He wandered among the gravestones, and it wasn't long before mysterious little eyes, bobbing around and jumping into his line of vision, began looking at him.

Yes, eyes! They were bluish, and they peeked at him from behind the stones, mostly in hiding. He saw them only fleetingly. He'd catch them out of the corner of his eye, mischievous little glowing orbs, accompanied by giggles of childish laughter. Each time he'd try to look at them directly, they would vanish, only to pop up somewhere else. Jim remembers: "That first time I went in by myself and started in a brave mood, but I came out of there plenty scared."

Jim was a firm believer after two or three visits to the graveyard, so he decided to take a couple of doubting friends on his next visit. They stationed themselves outside the gate and as they waited for the midnight hour, the two doubters began to lose their nerve. They were both scared; in fact, they didn't even want to venture inside.

The three looked in from the outside, and suddenly they saw many pairs of blinking blue eyes, darting around, accompanied by childish laughter. One of Jim's friends, completely astounded, couldn't wait to express his amazement and said a strong cuss word. At this, the little eyes turned from blue to an angry red! Apparently that word was enough for the little ghosts, and they all faded away. Jim and his friends decided they'd had enough for one evening and went home.

From Jim Dunbar's memories comes another story. On the north wall there is an ancient oak, he'll tell you, that actually talks to you. According to Jim—and others as well—the tree does talk, not in words, of course, but in movements. The trunk bends and sways when you talk to it, waving its branches in ways that seem to correspond to your words. Some have said they even see a face in the trunk! Pure imagination? Perhaps, because others cannot see it at all.

Far back in the southwest corner of the hoary, age-old Midway cemetery, there are two graves close together. The placement of these graves seems strange, because one is the resting place of a Confederate soldier, the other of a Union soldier. At times, say witnesses, the two appear physically on the ground above and break out into a fight! The two start out sitting on the grass playing cards, then have a disagreement that ends in a brawl.

12

The Reappearance
of Button Gwinnett

Midway/St. Catherine's Island

He's best known for being a signer of the Declaration of Independence. He's also known for the fact that his signature is so rare that it's worth thousands of dollars (that is, if you can find one). Button Gwinnett has a third distinction—he engaged in "pistols at dawn" and was killed in a bitter duel in 1777. That was a long time ago, but many will tell you that Button Gwinnett seems to still be lingering in Liberty County.

Gwinnett was reported to be tall and to command a rather noble appearance. Although polite and mild in his use of language, he had fatal flaws. He was irresponsible in his handling of money, quarrelsome, and said to be possessed of a scheming ambition and a false sense of honor.

Gwinnett had been a merchant in Charleston, but in 1765 he tired of that, sold out, and decided he would become a planter. He secured title to beautiful St. Catherine's Island on a long-term lease.

Button Gwinnett

He didn't use his land to its greatest agricultural potential, however, and managed his money poorly. He began borrowing from new sources to pay off old debts. He was constantly harassed by collectors. Foreclosure followed, and he lost possession of his island paradise.

This was a humbling experience for Gwinnett, but he bounced back. He became active in politics, first winning a seat in Georgia's Colonial Assembly, later being elected to the Continental Congress, which met in Philadelphia. While there, he voted for and signed the Declaration of Independence. Gwinnett returned to Georgia, and his prestige increased when he took part in a convention to frame a new provincial constitution. Then, early in 1777, he was named president of the Provincial Council.

Then a bitter feud developed, brought on by the envy and

hatred between two distinguished men: Gwinnett and Colonel Lachlan McIntosh, commander of the Continental Brigade. Such was their animosity that Gwinnett challenged McIntosh to a duel. Pistols were the chosen weapons. The adversaries faced off at dawn on May 16, 1777 near present-day Thunderbolt (in the Savannah area). Both duelists were wounded but Gwinnett's injury was more severe. The bullet shattered a bone in his upper leg. He contracted gangrene and died a few days later. He was just forty-five years old when Colonel McIntosh's bullet ended his life.

As a ghostly aftermath of the duel, Gwinnett's spirit is believed to haunt both Liberty County and St. Catherine's Island. In hushed tones, people will tell you that on dark nights, especially when a storm is threatening, the gallop of a fast horse can be heard above the rustling of the wind in the pines. But it's more than the drumming tattoo of just any horse. It's the phantom hoof beats of Chickasaw, Gwinnett's favorite saddle horse. Then you see him, a spectral horseman rushing past the old town of Midway on his way to his home on St. Catherine's. He heads for the island, disappears, then reappears near the wharf where his schooner, *Beggar's Benison,* was once moored. It's also been said that if you look seaward, you can make out the vessel itself, battling the waves. Indeed, the *Beggar's Benison* can be seen crossing the turbulent waters of the sound, carrying Gwinnett from the mainland to the St. Catherine's dock.

By the end of the nineteenth century, laws against dueling were toughened. Gentlemen began to realize that their old-fashioned codes of honor weren't so sacred after all, and dueling became a thing of the past. No one knows how many spirits of old duelists still stand at the ready in Georgia, fingering their dueling pistols with a caressing touch, then taking aim at an imaginary target. There must be lots of these entities, judging from the vast number of men who engaged in pistols at dawn. And one of these belligerent ghosts, surely, is the one and only Button Gwinnett.

The Racket in the Restaurant

Eulonia

Near the coastal town of Eulonia, there is a fine seafood restaurant that features more than just good food. Within its walls is an unseen entity that releases "Hey-I'm-here" reminders every now and then, like the calling card of someone who knows the place and has a proprietary feeling of ownership.

In 1995 Jackie Summers was called in to act as a trainer of personnel at the chain restaurant. Jackie, fully experienced in restaurant work and well qualified for the job, had been summoned due to the serious illness of Myrtle Parker, who was the manager at the time. The two worked together for a while, and Jackie helped with managerial duties. Sadly, only a short time later, Mrs. Parker passed away. She had suffered a stroke, then had been diagnosed with cancer.

The restaurant, located on a main highway, has a serene, peaceful pond and a small one-story house just behind it. The house, in a quiet, woodsy setting, has always been the property of the owner's family, and remains available for use by current managers. Mrs. Parker had lived there for thirteen years and had died there. The elderly Mr. Travis, founder of the restaurant and head of the clan that owned it, had also lived in the same house for a long time and also had passed away within its walls.

Jackie took over the duties of manager and moved into the little house. A short time later, things started happening! She began to hear nighttime noises in the house, mostly coming from the kitchen. There was the sound of glasses clinking and being moved about and of ice tinkling in the glasses. Now and then Jackie could hear the sound of a glass being set down on the counter. Jackie was really frightened when she recalled that her predecessor, Mrs. Parker, had been a heavy drinker!

But that wasn't all. Doors would frequently open and shut by themselves, and strange sounds would emanate from the yard. Mostly, however, the eerie sounds came from various parts of the house, especially the kitchen.

Meanwhile, a wide assortment of things had started happening in the restaurant too. Glasses and other containers would fall off tables, and the tops of pots and pans would fly off for no reason at all. Something put down in one place would not be found, but after a search (sometimes a long one), the item would be found in a completely different place.

One day Jackie was arranging time cards, and she carefully

wrapped a rubber band around them and left them on one of the booth tables. When the accountant asked, "Where are my time cards?" Jackie said, "Right there on that table." "Oh, no, they're not," came the answer. Sure enough, Jackie was shocked to find that they had disappeared. Jackie had not moved the time cards, and other employees had no idea how they had vanished. In this case, a long search at first revealed nothing, but finally the missing cards were located inside a metal cabinet.

One of the really puzzling and scary happenings took place after closing one night when only Jackie and the dishwasher were still on the job. An empty tea pitcher had been set on the table beside a large tea urn. Suddenly, the pitcher swished through the air and landed under the sink all the way across the room! "Why did you throw that?" yelled Jackie. "Not me. I didn't," said the dishwasher. Nothing was broken, but it scared the two of them.

Another time, a rack of glasses had been removed from the dishwashing machine and laid on a table. Jackie looked over at it— and it moved! It slid right off the table onto the floor. Only a few of the glasses were broken, but it made a horrible racket and put quite a scare into Jackie and the kitchen workers. That wasn't the only time a rack of glasses hit the floor. Waitresses have seen it happen at other times. The rack is always moved by an unseen hand and there is always minor damage to the glasses in the rack. Another more recent event involved a jar of seasoning that fell off a high shelf and landed with a loud *crack* on the grill.

All of these disturbances have convinced both Jackie and her kitchen staff that some*thing* is lingering and doing mischief in their restaurant. The number one suspect, naturally enough, is the former manager, Mrs. Parker.

Jackie often ponders something that might be significant. She recalls that the two people who passed away in the rear bungalow were involved in both the house and the restaurant. She wonders, Would earthbound spirits be summoned more readily from such a double tragedy of fate? In other words, are the pranks of this troublesome entity (showing all the attributes of a poltergeist) more pronounced because there were two mortals who departed from earthly spheres in the same nearby dwelling?

If this is true, however, then why do the activities of this spirit seem to be related to only one of the two mortals? The pranks seem to reflect the life and personality of Mrs. Parker. There is no reason why old Mr. Travis would want to rattle things in the house or disrupt the kitchen. He loved the whole place. But it's well known that Mrs. Parker resented some of Jackie's policies and ideas. This resentment flared during the brief interval when the two worked together. In fact, Jackie will admit today that they "locked horns" on different occasions. Is most of the ghost's damage done because of a certain seething hostility from the old days?

Nevertheless, the restaurant continues to do a fine business. Few of its satisfied customers know of the naughty ghost and the things she is doing to disturb the peace!

14

Leftover Spirits Walk Here

Liberty County

I t all happened in Liberty County . . . and it's still happening today!

The house in question is not an antiquated place; it's only three years old! But Jim and Meg Conover and their three dogs are certainly having encounters!

Strange disturbances started only a few months after the Conovers moved into the house in 1999. Meg's dad was visiting from West Virginia. One day, Meg looked into the dining room from the kitchen through a window in the wall between the two rooms. She knew her dad had been sitting there in a chair only a few moments before. Imagine Meg's surprise when she saw someone else sitting in the chair he had been occupying! "My God, what's Dad doing in his underwear?" she said out loud.

The sudden guest was tall, bare-chested, and naked except for a garment that looked like a loincloth wrapped around his waist. He was bare-headed with long, black, shoulder-length hair. These attributes, along with high cheekbones and a hooked nose, gave him the features of an American Indian. Meg kept staring, unbelievingly, until the apparition dissolved. All this time, her dad was nowhere in sight. (He was outside at the time.)

Meg was the only one who saw the Indian on that occasion, but others saw him at different times. Each time, Jim and Meg's three dogs—a pure-bred Doberman pinscher, a pure-bred Dalmatian, and a half-wolf half-dog mix—would growl and bark, but the Indian never said a word. Time and time again, he would walk silently through the house. Sometimes, as Meg watched him pass, he would turn his head and look at her. Predictably, when Meg or Jim would look through the house after one of his walks, he was nowhere to be found.

The Conover house is close to the Liberty Trail, a place where colonists, soldiers, slaves, and surely Indians were very much present at various times in the past. Historical markers line the trail. There was action here—gunfire and clashing swords, war whoops of Native Americans, and bloody combat, along with the cries of the wounded or dying and the pounding of horses' hooves as they made dashing pursuits, followed by a fugitive's capture or a thrilling escape. With so much heritage, it is not surprising that ghosts are walking the earth (and the floors of houses) in this area.

The Conovers have other ghosts too. They share their house

with a Civil War soldier who seems to be there to stay! The three dogs always sense the presence of the old soldier and set up a howling, noisy racket. During his first visitation, when the dogs didn't actually see him but only heard him, the dogs faced the closed back door and put on their best watch-dog performance. They sensed something approaching and set up a thunderous racket of barking and growling.

Suddenly there was a loud, fast rapping on the outside of the door. Meg remembers it well: "It sounded like maybe a riding crop striking the door." The loud *rap-rap-rap* sounded almost as though somebody outside wanted the dogs to shut up. In fact, they did. As soon as the knocking started, they immediately quieted down.

This was the Conovers' first hint of an old battlefield commander's presence. Two or three days later, they finally saw him. Jim and Meg were sitting in the living room when out of the kitchen walked a man in what was unmistakably a Civil War officer's uniform. He was solid, not filmy or transparent, all Confederate gray in color. There were two rows of buttons down his front, and he wore a high, stiff collar typical of a high-ranking officer but had no sword. There was a knotted sash with tassels around his waist. He wore high cavalry boots with spurs on the heels, and a standard field officer's hat with a Confederate emblem at the front.

"The Colonel," as Jim and Meg have come to call him, walked through the living room and into the guest room. He looked at everybody but didn't say a word. As for Jim and Meg, they were

shocked into silence and could only look at each other in disbelief. This was only the first of what would be many sightings of The Colonel. As Jim and Meg got more used to him, they began to realize he was a friendly spirit who had no unfriendly intentions. Each time they saw him, they would simply say, "Well, there goes The Colonel again!"

There is yet another entity in the Conover house, and this one is a poltergeist that moves things around and sometimes knocks things off tables and shelves. One time Meg was washing the dishes and her dad was watching TV. Suddenly an ornamental glass candleholder was knocked off its perch on the television set and landed on the floor. Nothing was damaged, but Meg and her dad figured maybe the ghost was upset because her dad, who had been visiting for about six months, was going back to West Virginia. The ghost didn't want to see him leave. "I am sure they get used to people and don't like it when folks either move in or move out," says Meg.

This naughty ghost likes to hide things, such as hairbrushes and books. A tempting area for the ghost is a large bed with pockets and shelves in its headboard. The spirit likes to throw things from the shelves onto the bed. On one occasion, Meg couldn't find two different TV remotes! How could they both disappear at once? Meg decided to give the ghost a taste of her anger, saying loudly, "I want them back!" Then she added, "I want them in five minutes!" Her shouts must have worked, for the remotes appeared just a bit later on a couch.

The poltergeist doesn't appear in human form. It appears as a blob about three or four feet high, sometimes black, at other times white or yellow. The entity is never seen distinctly but is cloudy or smoky.

Whatever these ghosts in the Conover household represent, they seem to be friendly and not malevolent in any way. Will they stay awhile? Nobody knows, but Jim and Meg don't seem to be too worried about it.

15

The Ghost Hung Out under the House

St. Marys

There was a crawl space beneath the old house. Why did the ghost make this his special headquarters?

The house was built around 1810 in St. Marys in the Queen Anne style, with several columns and a wraparound porch embellishing its all-white facade. The builder had done a fine job because even in 2001 it was solid and livable.

A number of owners in the early days included a corporate executive. A later tenant was a doctor who used the first floor for his office and waiting rooms and the second floor for his living quarters, including a second-floor kitchen. Still later, the first floor was used as a dentist's office. The house had been vacant for quite a while when the Maxwell family bought it in 1963. Charley Maxwell was a technician at the Gilman Paper Company, and he and his wife, Martha, had five children.

Even before they moved in, however, the Maxwells heard stories. People would warn them, "Don't buy that place—it's haunted!" There were tales of people on the street seeing shapes and figures in the windows while it was vacant. They saw flickering lights and heard strange noises. The house got quite a reputation.

Charley and Martha generally laughed these warnings off. But there was one tale that made Charley wonder if maybe there was something to the ghost stories after all. Mrs. Windsor, wife of Dr. Windsor, told Charley about something that happened when she and her husband lived there.

One hot summer day I came home, carrying two heavy bags of groceries, and I came staggering in the side door. I was hot and tired; in fact, I was just plain exhausted. Anyway, I started up the stairs with the two bags and got as far as the stair landing. Here I put my burdens down, saying "That's it!" I went into the guest room and flopped on the bed. I'll put away those groceries later, I told myself.

Well, I woke up two hours later and went back to the landing. Imagine my surprise when the groceries were not there! I looked in the kitchen, and there they were—all in place and neatly arranged just right on the shelves.

When my husband came home, I said to him, "Thanks, dear, for putting away the groceries for me."

"What do you mean?" he asked. "I did no such thing!"

At this, the two looked at each other, thunderstruck. Mrs. Windsor thought her husband had put the groceries away because no one else was home at the time and *everything was put away in perfect order.* But if he had not done it, then who?

Of course, that was part of the past—a long time ago. When the Maxwells assumed ownership, they looked forward to enjoying their house, forgetting, for a time, what other people were saying about it. They decided to remodel. In those days it was hard to get contractors, so Charley did the remodeling himself, mostly expanding the kitchen by removing an old wall and all the boards and partitions that went with it. He put down his hammer in the middle of a job one night—and someone, or something, moved it! He didn't find it until the next day, when it reappeared in the same place Charley had left it.

From then on, other things happened. A presence was making itself known with noises, thumps, and bangs. Things would mysteriously disappear. Then one day, something in the "really spooky" category happened.

Martha and her youngest son, Mike, were walking home from an errand. As they neared the house, their pet beagle, Beauregard, got very excited. He ran forward, barking and growling, and seemed to be especially interested in the crawlspace under the house, which at that time was open since the lattice had been removed.

What was Beauregard barking at? He ran all around the house in a wild state, but his attention was directed at that crawlspace. Martha and Mike thought it must be an animal, perhaps a squirrel, a raccoon, or maybe even an armadillo. But when they looked under the house, there was no animal. Instead, there was a sort of blob, a misty, foggy shape that had no particular form. The shape moved around, and then, to their amazement, it formed itself into the shape of a funnel and "poured" itself into the ground!

A short time later, Martha was bringing groceries in the side door. Once again Beauregard started barking wildly. Martha and the kids looked under the house and, sure enough, there was that grayish, foggy shape again. This time the dog's hackles were up as he stormed at the thing, but it dissolved away without forming itself into the funnel shape. The ghostly fog was seen once more, when the Maxwells' oldest daughter was walking home with two friends. They all saw the blob for a short time before it vanished.

Then there was the guitar episode, an amusing yet hair-raising happening in the Maxwell household. When oldest son Steve was a teenager, he took up the guitar, which he kept upstairs in his bedroom. One night he was watching TV with his parents downstairs in the living room. When his parents reminded him it was his bedtime, he willingly went up to his room.

Some time late, Charley and Martha, still downstairs, heard a guitar playing upstairs. Charley scrambled up the stairs to find out why Steve was playing his guitar instead of sleeping. He was dumbfounded to find the boy sound asleep—and his guitar in a corner several feet away!

Who was playing? Steve's parents questioned him the next morning, asking, "What time did you go to bed?" He answered, "Just when you told me to." The mysterious late-night guitar strumming remains a mystery.

On the very spot of the house before 1810 stood a log cabin that housed a grocery store downstairs and living quarters for the owners upstairs. Digging down a bit into the ground beneath their house, the Maxwells have found a number of old bottles (some valuable) but no clues to the identity of their ghost. And as far as they are aware, no one has ever died on the premises.

The Maxwells have lived in their house for almost forty years. It's been a happy time, living with what they consider a friendly spirit, one who means them no harm and even (at times) displays a sense of humor.

16

Coastal Visitors
of Bygone Years

Jekyll Island

When Ruby Ryscamp looked into the dining room of that old inn, it was a magical experience in her life.

The large building on Jekyll Island had been a sort of "wayside inn" for generations. In its time it had hosted parties and conventions. Now, in December 1999, Ruby and her friends, headquartered at a nearby condo, were visiting the old hostelry while on a carefree vacation. They were interested in shopping and in discovering the lore and history of the area. In a fine mood, the four of them, happy and chatting, wandered through the lobby.

Ruby came to the dining room. She took a single step past the doorway. "I stood, for a moment, just inside the door," she explained later. "Only a very few diners were there at that hour."

Then came a tremendous déjà vu experience. She remembers feeling "three jolts," along with a sensation of being "pulled forward." Suddenly the scene before her was different. Guests wearing twentieth-century attire filled the room, sitting at a great many tables. The men were in formal, dark suits; the women in long dresses, shawls, lacy collars, and lots and lots of jewelry. Ruby noticed the jewelry especially. They were all elegantly dressed and had the look of wealthy people.

"I looked down at myself, and I, too, was wearing a long dress, whereas I had not been wearing it before!" Now came the goose bumps, and a jumble of thoughts ran through her mind, the foremost being, I must, in some way, have been here at some bygone time.

Ruby continued to stare, transfixed. The waiters were the only ones standing, and they wore dark jackets with tails. One of them was carrying a tray holding a large, domed dish cover that appeared to be silver. The room itself had also changed. The walls, plain before, had changed to a textured appearance, not unlike old-fashioned wallpaper. There were lots of heavy, golden drapes around the windows and fireplace, and the lighting was very subdued, so that the room took on a dark, romantic appearance.

Ruby now had strong feelings, not only of having been here before, but also of how anxious she would be to come back to this place again. Her trance lasted a full minute and didn't end until one of her friends grabbed her arm and called out, "Ruby! What in the world is the matter with you?"

Ruby came to her senses. Pale as a ghost, she tried to tell the others what had happened. Predictably, they found the story hard to believe. Then, going back with the gang, Ruby, pale and shaken, managed to go on a shopping trip and somehow make it through the day. Locked in her mind, however, was a singular yearning to search for more clues to this strange occurrence and to return to this area.

And Ruby did return to the island. In the early summer of 2001, she stayed with a friend in rented quarters, the top floor of an old apartment that had a historical, weathered, lived-in appearance. Just after their arrival, the two women were on a small balcony outside their apartment, admiring a pleasant view, when Ruby looked back through the glass doors and gasped at what she saw: "Look! There's a woman in our apartment!"

Their surprise guest was remarkably well dressed and beautiful. She seemed to be around thirty years old, and they noticed that she was slender, of medium height, with light brown hair softly done up in an old-fashioned bouffant. Her dress looked like a moiré fabric in peachy-pink with a tinge of brown—a lovely, soft color. It was close-fitting, but at the waist it became fuller, and there was something at the back—"not a bustle," said Ruby, more like a "gathering" or a bow. Ruby took note of ivory lace at her neckline and at the ends of her three-quarter-length sleeves. She didn't remember that the apparition wore any rings or other jewelry.

The woman stood in a statuesque pose, smiling at them in a serene and peaceful way. They smiled back. Then Ruby turned to her friend momentarily. When she turned back, the figure was gone. When they talked about it later, the Ruby and her friend remembered that the woman was a solid apparition with no semblance of transparency. They could not see her whole body, since it was partly hidden by a table, but they had a feeling she was wholly visible..They never saw their lovely guest again.

Perhaps the strange lady was the spirit of the wife or companion of a wealthy gentleman who vacationed at Jekyll during another era. Or. . . . Something flashed through Ruby's mind. If I had been here in another lifetime, perhaps that was *me* when I was here, she thought. Could it be?

The Desperate Fight in the Old Inn

There were other ghostly events in the old inn where Ruby Ryscamp had her déjà vu experience. Perhaps the most spine-chilling was the one that happened the night the police were called.

The story comes from Bob Murphy of Camden County, whose father, Dave, was a patrolman for the Georgia State Police. Bob had heard plenty of yarns growing up because Dave loved to tell the family about the incidents and arrests of his duty years. One of the most interesting tales took place around 1974, when Dave was called to Jekyll Island one night to check on a disturbance. Custodians at the old inn reported the loud noises of a scuffle in the lobby. They hadn't seen anything in the dim light, but it sounded like two men going at it with everything they had—a really fierce standoff. There were howls, groans, cussing, and the sound of bodies rolling on the floor!

At this time, the old inn was fairly inactive, with only a few rooms occupied. It was a dark night and the lobby was dimly lit, so it was hard to see anything. When Dave arrived, he began to hear noises as he approached the foyer. There could be no doubt that a ferocious battle was going on. The sound of bodies crashing into the furniture and struggling on the floor was unmistakable.

Upon reaching the scene of strife, Dave turned on his flashlight. He saw nothing, but at the instant his light went on, the noises stopped on the first floor, only to be heard immediately coming from the second floor. It was eerie—no humans, no sign of the fight, no more sounds of battle on the first floor. The scuffling sounds had shifted to the second floor lobby, directly above.

So Dave went upstairs. The noises got louder as he climbed the stairs but when he reached the second floor and shined his flashlight at the trouble spot, the sounds stopped again and shifted to the third floor! So Dave climbed one more flight of stairs. This time, as he directed his light around the third floor hallway, the sounds again disappeared . . . and went *downstairs*. He heard them, strong and definite, from where he had just come on the second floor!

It was about this time that Dave began to suspect he was dealing with the supernatural. It was with a sigh of exasperation that he started down to the second floor lobby. As he descended the stairs, he said to himself, "Don't know why I'm going down here. I know what I'm going to find."

Sure enough, when he reached the second floor and directed his light, the sounds went back to the first floor. Upon arriving at ground level, Dave was in such a state of disgust that he didn't even make a search. It was hopeless, he told himself—no way to find this elusive ghost! He walked out of the old building, deciding, No more ghost hunts for me!

There has never been an explanation for the desperate fight in the old inn. It remains a mystery.

17

The Haunts
of Dungeness

Cumberland Island

John F. Kennedy Jr. knew what he was doing when he chose Cumberland Island for his wedding. The Kennedy party wanted "no hordes of people" and "no helicopters hovering overhead."

This barrier island at the Georgia-Florida border is eighteen miles long, about a mile wide, and as restful a getaway as you could find. Temperatures are moderate, semitropical breezes stir the palms and palmettos, and wildlife abounds. The island is home to armadillos, bobcats, alligators, feral pigs, white-tailed deer, and the famous wild horses of Cumberland.

Truly, this is a land of coastal magic. It's so quiet—that's what strikes you first—a hush that's somehow deeper than silence, a tranquil wooing of the senses that makes you glad to be away from the noise and bustle of life in the fast lane.

Through the years, Cumberland has been occupied by Indians,

Ruins of the old Carnegie Mansion, Dungeness
(photo courtesy of Bill Jenkins)

the Spanish, planters and their slaves, pirates, Confederates—and the wealthy. One of our Revolutionary leaders, Nathaniel Greene, built a plantation here in the late 1780s. Other notables established residences, most prominently the family of Thomas Carnegie, brother of millionaire steel manufacturer Andrew Carnegie. The Carnegies built a huge brick mansion in the late 1800s, naming it Dungeness.

There are ghostly tales on Cumberland, and one of the most often told concerns this grand old mansion. The place is now in ruins, having burned in 1959 and never been fully restored. It's a major stop for sightseers, however. When they walk the quiet woodland trail from the dock, escorted by a knowledgeable naturalist guide, they are awed by the ruins, still majestic, still casting a spell.

As visitors approach the long, straight driveway, guarded by two concrete posts supporting a lovely overhead arch, their guide may tell them about the accident that happened here long ago—and its ghastly aftermath. At various times, when they least expect it, he'll tell you, today's visitors will hear the creaking of wooden wheels going down the driveway. Then, something else is heard. . . .

Long ago, during the Carnegie era, so goes the tale, a carriage filled with guests was on its way to the mansion for a party. The carriage careened out of control and flipped over on its side. Ever since, spirits of the guests killed in the mishap have, at odd times, cried out in misery. Their wails of agony, combined with the squeaking of the old wagon wheels, create a dismal harmony of doom and despair. Could it be that these lost souls are still trying to get to the party?

Toward the sea, only a few hundred yards down the road from the mansion, is the old carriage house. It, too, has a supernatural tale to tell. More than eighty years old, the two-story tabby building has a steeply pitched gray roof and several dormer windows on the second floor. In the old days, the carriage house was a stowage area for saddles, harnesses, bridles—all things related to horsemanship. Now, its first floor is home to saws, tractors, and other mechanical equipment for maintaining the island's paths and landscaping. The second floor is just an attic where carriage parts roost, gathering dust. No one goes up there—*ever*—and the door is kept locked. That's why it was so shocking when Fred Carver, a maintenance worker, saw her in one of the upstairs dormer windows!

She had a pale face and long, dark hair and wore what seemed to be a white, flowing dress. Carver, even in his shook-up state, couldn't get over one thing about her. He noticed something most unusual about her eyes. "They appeared to be merely dark holes in her face," he said. "Big, dark holes."

This was not the only time he saw the mysterious woman. She appeared to him several times, and each time her appearance seemed to change slightly. He found out from coworkers that they also had seen her, and all the descriptions seemed to match, even those about the changes in her appearance. It was Fred Carver, however, who gave the most graphic descriptions.

Once, reported Carver, she moved past the dormers in a sort of slow parade, and he held his breath as he waited for her to appear at the next window. She would glance out for a few seconds at each window, then move on. As she moved along, her image evolved into a cloudy mass, becoming less and less the form of a human being. Sometimes, when in her well-defined shape, she also appeared to rise.

Carver remembers that anytime he walked alongside the building, the watcher at the window would move also, going from one window to the next as if following him. This gave him a creepy feeling, and he wouldn't be able to get the thought of her image out of his mind for quite a while.

Workers in the carriage house have also reported noises at odd times and even vague shapes moving around in the yard, especially in the vicinity of the other small outbuildings. The shapes look like the apparitions of people, they say, but these forms can never be seen clearly enough to be identified in any way. On one occasion, a workman in the day crew was working on one of the Ranger Station automobiles. Suddenly he heard a loud "Hey!" over his shoulder. When he turned to look, there was no one there.

It's likely the second floor of the carriage house was once living quarters for the families of the men who took care of the Carnegies' horses. This would have been usual in the nineteenth century. But who was the woman at the window? Was she, indeed, a wife or daughter of one of the carriage employees? If so, there is no indication of such a woman living or dying at this location.

18

Are Great Writers
the Resident Ghosts?

Jekyll Island

I n the morning, the book store manager enters his store, only to
find his stock scattered and rearranged. During the night, a hidden "something" has come in and made some big changes—moving
books to different places throughout the store. But that's not all. The
same naughty presence has been known to grab books off the shelves
and throw them at browsers!

George Avis, former manager of the store on Jekyll Island,
knows what it means to get frustrated. He hated to come in and find
books scattered around, but he always grinned in a spirit of good
humor, believing the bookstore had a friendly spirit guardian.

George was quite sure it was a female spirit. One afternoon he
was upstairs, rearranging shelves, when a shape appeared at the end
of the hallway. What George saw was not a clear figure but the indistinct form of a person, and it was beckoning to him to come near-

er. Naturally, he thought it was his assistant, signaling him to help her do something. So George called out, "I'll be there in a minute."

After finishing his tasks, he went downstairs and asked the assistant what she had wanted.

"I don't know what you mean," she answered.

"You know," he said, "when you motioned for me upstairs."

"What on earth are you talking about?"

She kept insisting she had not been upstairs, and at this point George told her exactly what had transpired. His helper was getting more and more unsettled as the tale unfolded. "One more word," she said defiantly, "and I'll grab my purse and leave this instant."

But that's not the only strange occurrence that took place in the store. Loud bumps and thumps are heard, mostly from upstairs. The ghost also cracked a quarter-inch-thick plate of glass on one of the main room display tables.

Walter Rogers Furness built the building in 1890. Over the years, it changed hands often and had several different owners. Records show that the building was actually moved three times, the last move taking it from the riverside to its present location. It's also interesting that around 1930 it became an infirmary. Could this partly explain the ghost? Could it be that earthbound spirits of sick or dying patients are still hanging around? Are they unhappy that their old resting place is now a retail store? Are they disrupted by book store customers who disturb their peace and quiet?

This may be, but it's at odds with what long-time manager

George Avis jokingly said on many occasions: "Our unseen guests are the spirits of old journalists." In fact, a sign in one section of the store says: "This shop is haunted by the ghosts of great writers and . . . ?" Hoping to pick up a clue on this, George, after some especially loud noises one day, decided to give a direct challenge to his noisy antagonist. Loudly he called out, "What the dickens is that? Is that you, Charles Dickens?"

The joke was greeted with total silence.

19

The Spirits of Sapelo

Sapelo Island

O n Sapelo Island there is a glorious interval when the sun's rays gain strength and clear away the shrouds of night. Some might call this dawn but to Sapelo residents of African heritage, it's "dayclean."

Yes, *dayclean*. There's a sort of happy, melodious ring to it, a time when the day is new and the world is made fresh again.

In her best-selling book, *God, Dr. Buzzard, and the Bolito Man,* Cornelia Bailey talks of ghosts, but she doesn't call them ghosts. She calls them spirits, and if you are wise, you don't underestimate the many spirits of Sapelo: "They are just as real as any flesh-and-blood person, so they are quite powerful, and there is such a thin veil between this world and the next that they can make themselves known. And even though you wanted to believe that all of them were good, a spirit could be good or bad depending on the nature of

The Spirits of Sapelo are on guard.
(photo courtesy of Bill Jenkins)

the person they had been."

According to Cornelia, following the beliefs of her African ancestors, when a person dies the body goes to the grave and the soul rests in peace. But the *spirit* remains on earth. "So, you see, the spirit is always here. It stays until it is reconnected to the body on judg-ment day."

To today's visitor, Sapelo Island is a mystic, quiet place. Owned largely by the Department of Natural Resources (DNR), it has a rather foreboding appearance when approached on the island ferry. After a half-hour boat ride (no causeway or bridge), you first see the island as just a wooded "mound," looking a bit ominous, with no sign of habitation. Only when you get closer do you see that it has people and such things as autos and trucks, mostly owned by DNR employees. Wild and unspoiled, the verdant scenery surrounds you. Hanging over it all like a calm, protective curtain is that blanket of silence, not without an air of mystery and wonder. . . .

Let's go back to the early 1970s. The scene is an old, two-story house on the west side of Sapelo in an area now set aside as the Richard J. Reynolds Wildlife Refuge. The place has many secrets, but we'll start with an account by Bob Comstock when he was a guest here. Bob was a young marine biologist at the time, and the fellow he was visiting in that secluded woodland area was a wildlife biologist. Both worked for the Department of Natural Resources. Along with other DNR staffers, Bob had temporary quarters in the department's research boat, moored at the Sapelo dock. He would frequently visit other DNR people on the island, sometimes staying over weekends.

One weekend, Bob was assigned to the southernmost bedroom on the second floor. He will never forget what happened in the middle of that very first night. He was awakened by a mysterious presence. A woman, dressed all in white (a dress or maybe a gown, he says), stood at the foot of his bed. She had long blond hair. She simply stood there and stared at him without saying anything.

"At first," remembers Bob, "I thought it was the wife of one of the other guys, coming in from another bedroom." He thought it mighty strange, but then he just ignored her, rolled over and closed his eyes. He didn't wake up until morning; by then, the apparition was gone. Bob had no other experiences in that house or anywhere else on Sapelo, but he'll tell you that a wildlife technician who owned the house previously had many experiences. This man had plenty of stories, and he loved to tell them! He would often wake up in the morning and find a chair on top of the dining room table! He would also frequently find windows and doors wide open that he was sure he had shut the night before.

Other bizarre tales can be told by Fred Dowling, who lived on Sapelo in the late 1970s. Fred, a DNR official now stationed in Brunswick, recalls the day he came home for lunch after working all morning. His wife was not at home, and he thought she had gone shopping. Fred started making a sandwich for himself in the kitchen. Suddenly, from upstairs, he heard the unmistakable sound of furniture being dragged around. Well, he said to himself, she must be up there, changing the room around. He went on making lunch. Then the sounds, to his surprise, got louder and seemed to come from different parts of the upper story. Thinking that was odd, he went up to investigate.

Imagine his surprise when there was no one up there—and all the furniture was perfectly in place! No sign of any disturbance. Fred was mystified and kept looking around, sure that his wife was up there somewhere. But, no, she wasn't. At this point, Fred's wife drove up, back from her errand. He told her all about his experience. Neither one had an explanation for the mysterious sounds.

Jeff Preston of the DNR lives in the house today. And Jeff, along with his family, has had supernatural experiences too! He likes to give visitors a bit of background. The house, he says, was built by Howard Coffin, the Detroit auto executive who is best known as the developer of Sea Island. When Coffin owned Sapelo, he made big changes on the island in the early 1900s. Jeff's house was one of three said to have been built around 1917 for three sisters. Later, it became an old folks' home, and many people died there.

Jeff's daughter, Sally, who occupied the southernmost bedroom on the second floor, is probably the one with the most vivid experiences of the supernatural. One day Sally looked out her window and saw a woman in a white dress in the nearby field bordering the marsh. The woman wore a wide, white hat and her dress was old-fashioned, "like the clothing people wore back around the nineteen twenties," Sally says. The woman appeared to be kneeling rather than standing. Sally reported the sighting to her parents, but the apparition has not been seen again around the house or yard.

Sally and her younger sister, Margie, will never forget the time they heard a "concert" of old-time music from the attic. Sally heard it first, and when she woke up Margie, they both listened, wide-eyed and trembling. The music flowed down from the attic early in the morning while the girls were still in bed. Sally, who is quite precise in her knowledge of the eras of music, says, "It was definitely not the Big Band era, not music of the thirties or forties, but more like the dance rhythms of the twenties, or maybe earlier."

As the sisters listened, they noticed that along with the music came the unmistakable sound of dancing feet. Impossible as it may seem, it sounded like people were having a party up there. The two girls, now really frightened, ran to their parents' bedroom. "It was *loud*," they said, describing their experience. But by the time Jeff and his wife, Grace, got out of bed and investigated, the sounds had stopped.

Sally also recalls how her bed would get "sat on" every morning. Regular as clockwork, she says. "It seemed to happen when I was half awake. I would sense another presence in the room, hear faint squeaking noises, and then feel that someone sat right down on the other side of the bed! It happened over and over again."

There are two other events that Jeff Preston can remember. In one case, daughter Margie, while outside the house, saw a man inside looking out through a window. She came in and asked her grandmother, who was working in the kitchen, "Who is that man standing in the window?" Her grandmother shook her head, informing her that there was no one else in the house at the time.

"But I just saw him in the window," said Margie.

Other family members were surprised when they heard Margie's story because Margie sounded so positive in describing the man. Finally, they pulled out a family album. As they looked through the pictures, Margie identified an older family relative, now deceased. "That's him. That's who I saw," she said.

Another time, Jeff's sister-in-law, then visiting, arose from bed extremely shook up. "I think someone was in that bed with me!" she gasped to Jeff and Grace. It seems she heard the sound of someone breathing close to her ear, and it wouldn't go away!

20

The Haunted Rocking Chair

Liberty County

That rocking chair seemed to have a mind of its own. It rocked by itself. And since it was the seat Stan Rhodes' father had always taken when watching television, could it be . . . that Dad was *still in it?*

Stan and his mother, Grace, had the uncanny feeling they were sharing their house trailer with a ghost. Dave Rhodes passed away in 1993. He left his favorite chair as a sort of memento to his wife and son in the single-wide trailer that was their home in Liberty County. They watched it rock by itself most every night, and although Stan always saw it empty, his mom could see much more! To her, it was still occupied by Dave, smiling and watching television, just about every night when she looked into the living room from her bedroom. There he was, an off-white apparition, sitting in his underwear and in his semi-solid state, whitish and glowing, she could see the rocking chair right through him. "One explanation for his

appearance there," says Grace, "is the simple fact that I didn't move that chair around. I left it where it was."

Stan says, "I looked at that chair and although I never did see his figure there, I would see and feel things that seemed to be directly related to him." Actually, Grace would see Dave in two places—sitting in his chair and also reflected in the glass of the TV set. When she would get out of bed and walk toward the living room, however, he would fade away. Try as she might, Grace could not get any closer to his image.

Stan recalls that his father was an insomniac, staying up late and hardly ever going to bed at a reasonable time. Since Dave's death, reminders of Dave have lingered. For example, he had a habit of leaving the TV and the light over the stove on when he went to bed. He would give his rocking chair a few final rocks and head off to bed. Stan and Grace would turn everything off at night, including the light over the stove. But when they got up in the morning, the TV and the light would be on. Sometimes Stan would get up during the night and walk into the living room, only to find the light and the TV on—and the rocking chair rocking!

One night Stan and his girlfriend, Julie, were sitting on the floor, watching TV at about 2:00 A.M. Suddenly a sort of misty, foggy cloud appeared, rising against the wall under a picture of Dave. This was unusual in itself, but what happened next was truly amazing. They could see Dave's name spelled out in the cloud, just below his picture. The name was not written on the wall, it was *in the mist.* The name Dave Rhodes appeared as though drawn with a finger, and what a weird sight—similar to the effects of black, or ultraviolet, light.

Julie had an interesting experience one night when she was sitting alone in front of the TV. Julie was kind of upset about something and remembers, "I was sitting there and suddenly somebody tugged on my hair.. When there was another (harder) tug, I got up and jumped into bed. I was scared and didn't know what to do. I was shaking. Was it *him,* Stan's dad?" Julie wonders if the mysterious hair pull was a sort of "no-no" because she had been angry that night.

Besides the actual sightings of Dave, other things happened. There were strange marks on the wall of the trailer, Grace says, that wouldn't go away no matter how hard she scrubbed. "People would tell me they were blood stains." Also, Grace would come in from work and put her keys on the kitchen table. In the morning, the keys would be gone, only to appear later in the bathroom or maybe on top of the washing machine. "It was like he was playing tricks on me!"

She is convinced he was there since shortly after his death. "Yes, he's been watching over me. He's been with me for a long time, because we were very close."

Grace didn't work for six months after Dave died "because it just tore me up." And she didn't dispose of that rocking chair for a long, long time. Though she lives in a new home, Grace has memories, and she puts them into words well: "Every time I saw him I was comforted."

21

The Return of the Polo Player

Cumberland Island

It must have been a terrific impact when the horseman hit the low-hanging branch of the oak tree. The scene was Cumberland Island around the early 1900s, and the rider, a polo player, had been at an evening party at the old Carnegie mansion, Dungeness (see Chapter 16). According to the story, which has been passed on for years, the polo player was unhappy at the party because they ran out of his favorite beverage. Not a man to drink the "wrong stuff," he decided, in his semi-intoxicated state, to ride off to get more. He staggered to his horse and climbed unsteadily into the saddle.

The fellow knew the only place to get a refill was the nearby servants' quarters just down the road. In careless haste, he spurred his mount to a gallop, then, not fully in command of his equilibrium, dashed ahead in the darkness. The huge oak had no sympathy for the horseman. His progress was halted—permanently—by a

Oak branches, a hazard to horsemen at Cumberland Island.
(photo courtesy of Bill Jenkins)

thick, projecting limb that crossed his path at just the right height. He never saw it in the dark. When his head hit the branch with a terrible jolt, he was thrown from his horse and killed instantly.

For years afterwards, folks on Cumberland talked about this tragic accident. The rider had been an island guest who played polo, one of the recreational activities promoted by the Carnegies. Polo was a popular spectator sport for years, and the field was adjacent to the mansion. It was probably around World War II that interest in the noble equine sport faded.

One evening in the early 1990s, Janice Hanson, a naturalist and ornithologist for the National Park Service, was relaxing in one of the buildings. It had been a busy day of escorting bird lovers on a field trip, keenly observing many species, some of them rare. She was talking with two of her associates in the living room of the old wooden structure, which had been servants' quarters back in the Carnegie days.

Suddenly, Janice saw a man descend the stairs from the second floor. She noticed that he seemed young and athletic and had a very pale face. Wearing a white shirt and dark pants, he walked past them in silence, then went out the door.

"Who in the world was that man?" asked Janice.

"What do you mean?"

"The . . . the fellow who just came down the stairs."

Her coworkers didn't understand. They hadn't seen anything. One of them said, "Can't be! We are the *only* ones here tonight." While Janice described the fellow, they looked dumbfounded. However, one of the staff workers, after deep thought, said cautiously, "You . . . you *may* have seen the polo player!"

"What?"

"Well, these buildings, generally known as the barracks, are now used for visitors and guest chambers. But in the old days, they were servants' quarters. Well, this polo player was killed one night, coming over here from the mansion. They say he was searching for some liquor, and ever since there have been stories that he is still lurking in or around this very building!"

Janice was thunderstruck. "But why was I the only one who saw him?"

There was no answer, and the talk went on, about how he died a violent death when he ran into a branch of a giant oak tree. And all he was doing was leaving the party to get more supplies.

"Where was the polo field?" Janice asked.

"Well, we aren't sure since it was so long ago. But the most likely place was on the far (western) side of Dungeness where there was an old pergola, covered over now. It was a sort of arbor, a walkway with an open roof, flowered over with climbing vines. Near it, there is still a big, open space devoid of trees. Most likely that's where the playing field was."

The talk drifted to other things, but Janice couldn't forget the white-faced man who had walked through the room. She remembered how he had made no sound at all. "It could have been a ghost," someone said, and it gave her the shivers.

Another time, Janice had a different experience in that same building. She was staying there during a storm, and a loud clap of thunder woke her up. Glancing out the bedroom window, she saw a bright red light glowing in the darkness only a short distance away. It was round and reminded her "of the taillight on a car," except that it was bigger and higher, perhaps thirty or forty feet in the air.

Janice wanted to call someone, to talk about this light, perhaps to show it to somebody else. However, she was alone that night in the old barracks building. In days to come, she described the uncanny red light to several people, but no one could offer any explanation.

On another part of the island, you'll find Plum Orchard Mansion, formerly owned by other members of the Carnegie family. Although quite old, it is still a stately, white-pillared place with a large, open porch. This dwelling has its share of ghost stories too. A Department of Natural Resources ranger told Janice that once when he was alone in Plum Orchard, he heard the unmistakable sound of the dumbwaiter moving! This just can't be, he told himself. But there was no mistaking the noise of the old dumbwaiter starting from the kitchen and going up, making a stop at each floor, then going back down again. After a short pause, it started anew and did the same thing all over again!

The history of Cumberland Island includes exploration, triumphs, tragedies, odd personalities, and bloody violence. During the War of 1812, British soldiers captured the island and, in an effort to weaken Southern economy, tried to lure slaves away from the plantations, promising them freedom and transportation to certain British colonies. Civil War–era blockade runners used the nearby inlets for refuge. During World War II, Navy planes made emergency landings on the beaches—and some crashed here. With such a mixture of history—and mystery—there would seem to be plenty of logical reasons for discarnate entities to remain for a long, long time.

22

The Ghost Horse
of Jekyll Island

Jekyll Island

I t's an amazing tale, a story of a horse that was noble and, people
said, endowed with supernatural traits. The scene was Jekyll
Island, historic barrier island of Georgia about the time of the War
Between the States. Jekyll was a lush, wild oasis, and the only way
you could get there was by boat.

During the war, the picturesque island could not be defended
against Union gunboats, so the frightened and sometimes panic-
stricken plantation families knew they had to leave. As they departed, they freed their livestock into deserted pastures and fields, where
the animals could forage at their convenience. Later, however, with
the war over, returning families found to their dismay that Jekyll was
overcome with wild horses, hogs, and cattle that needed to be
rounded up.

Standing resolutely in the forefront of the band of wild horses was a beautiful young stallion, pure white and fleet of foot. People would see the animal wandering, often on Jekyll's broad and scenic beach. There were several attempts to capture him, but none were successful.

One of the horse's favorite habits was to trot, then break into a canter along the beach, his long white mane and tail flowing in the ocean breeze. The story goes that at the slightest hint of pursuit, he would give a loud and defiant neigh and make tracks for the woods.

As time went on and nothing could be done to catch the elusive horse, he became more and more of an irritation to the plantation owners. After all, they were trying to reclaim their once-productive land. How could they do this when the mystery horse, often accompanied by a few equine pals, would romp freely, trampling newly planted fields and jumping fences with careless abandon? It was a frustrating time for the planters.

The landowners, angry and determined, resolved that the horse must be caught at all costs. "We must organize a special hunt to get him," they said. They were dead serious, and soon a posse of mounted men was formed, with a pack of bloodhounds to help them. These hunters did not wish to kill the horse, for they had too much respect for him. They favored catching him and transporting him to another location. With this in mind they set out and, hunting near the ocean, soon spotted tracks. The hounds erupted in full cry. The chase was on!

After a short interval they saw their quarry up ahead. The white stallion was dashing down the beach, heading south toward the Cumberland Island end of Jekyll. His pursuers followed, scattering and breaking into small groups, then approaching from different points to cut off any hope of escape.

The hunters were relentless. Every time the fleeing horse tried to double-back or cross the island with a dash through the woods, a rider would stop him and drive him back to the beach. The horse, now tiring and feeling himself trapped, came to the southern tip of Jekyll. He rounded this southernmost point and came to a bald bluff, facing the mainland and overlooking the main channel. It is deep water here, but the water becomes shallower as the channel stretches toward the marsh lying between the island and the mainland. The horse mounted this bluff, closely pursued by the hunters and their hounds. Again he attempted to double-back, but his way was blocked by several pursuers, some of whom had come through the woods to head him off. In desperation, he turned to face his tormentors.

It was then that a boat, rowed by two plantation workers, approached from around the point. A second boat appeared down the channel a few hundred yards away. What happened next was probably to be expected. The valiant steed, knowing he was cornered, leaped over the edge, hitting the deep-channel water with a splash, and began swimming straight toward the marsh. It looked like he might get away, but at this point the angry hunters called to the men in the boats, "A hundred dollars to the boat that captures the white horse!"

Thus encouraged, the two boats surged forward. But somehow there was a reserve of strength in the fiery animal. Before the nearest boat could reach him, he gained the shallows and was seen floundering through the grass and mud of the marsh.

The hunters, watching the drama in frustration, saw the white horse struggle across the strip of marsh and approach the lagoon beyond. He was in the act of plunging into this lagoon when a long, dark object appeared in front of him. Rearing backwards with a wild neigh of terror, he fell in the muddy depths as another and another dark form surrounded him.

"The alligators got him!" gasped the leader of the posse, then added, "Had I dreamed that such would happen, I, for one, would never have joined in this fruitless chase." The other men seemed to agree, as a pall of sadness swept over them.

For many years, that sandy bluff has been called Horse Leap, but that's only part of the story. For a long time afterwards, folks claimed that the stallion's neigh could be heard when the wind howled through the live oaks and palm trees. Then, too, during storms, people would swear they saw a galloping phantom racing up the beach. At times his image was vague or transparent, but it was surely a white stallion, his long mane flying. And when islanders would gaze into the channel or across the ocean waters, they would swear they saw a plume in the midst of the waves. Sometimes they could make out a white body and part of a white tail too.

The superstitious plantation workers would whisper, "See, yonder in de marsh grass, de white hoss o' Jekkle." At other times, the workers from the cotton and rice fields would huddle close to the fire and say, "Heah dat? Trouble in de land. De white hoss of Jekkle's whickerin'."

23

Phantom Trails on Tybee Island

Tybee Island

Today, Tybee Island, just southeast of Savannah and the northernmost of the Georgia barrier islands, provides a mixture of fun, recreation, and history. At Tybee there's boating, sailing, a fishing pier, and the historic Tybee Lighthouse and Museum. The cooling breezes of Savannah Beach and the ever-present lure of hidden heritage offer a welcome respite for coastal inhabitants and out-of-town visitors. In particular, the North Beach area has a fascinating military history, along with beautiful dunes, bathing beaches, and a restful park. From the shore, there's a pleasing view of Daufuskie and Hilton Head Islands. Here, too, you can watch mammoth container ships plowing the waters of Savannah Harbor.

This north end of Tybee has been strategically important for hundreds of years. The American government ordered construction of a stronghold here in 1896 as part of an overall system of coastal defenses. It was first called Fort Tybee, then Camp Graham. In 1899, a presidential proclamation changed the name to Fort Screven in honor of General James Screven, a Revolutionary War hero who was killed in action near Midway, Georgia, in 1778. The fort was especially busy during the Spanish-American War and remained an active military post until 1945. Thus, military personnel have occupied this site through three wars, the Spanish-American War and both World Wars.

It was in the early 1990s that Gloria Watson was working as a chambermaid at the Savannah Beach Nursing Home in the Ft. Screven area of North Tybee. Gloria had always felt chilled and uncomfortable when people told her that a morgue had originally been at this location.

Working with another woman one day, Gloria was folding sheets in the laundry room when she had the uncanny feeling that someone was behind her. She kept looking back toward the door to the room. She commented to her coworker, "I feel like someone is there. Someone is watching us!"

The laundry room was situated low in the post hospital, almost underground, with a screen door to the outdoors. Suddenly Gloria turned and was shocked to see a man's figure go though the screen door without opening it. It was a shadowy form, dark and ominous, and not clearly defined—a sort of "gray man," as spelled out in some ghost literature. Without saying a word, he walked through the screen door, passed the two women, and vanished into a wall.

Gloria was quick to ask her partner, "Did you see that?"

"Did *you* see that?"

Later, Gloria verified that the man in gray wore clothes that were hard to make out but she knew they were not modern clothes. Although she saw no trace of medals, pins, or buttons, his clothing seemed to have a military cut. Also, she recalls that the sudden intruder was just a bit under six feet in height, wore no hat, and was not old but, rather, quite young with quick movements.

Although the man in gray was never seen again in the nursing home, a second, similar ghost was seen at a nearby location and reported to Gloria by a friend. It seems that, overlooking the fort area, there was a crescent, or semi-circular ridge of land, that used to be called Officer's Row. It was here that a row of fine, comfortable houses were built for the fort's officers. When Gloria's friend lived in one of these homes, she told this tale: "I was in my living room one day, and I looked up to see this man in gray go right through the door without opening it. But the image I saw was only half a man. I only saw the top part of him, and there was no indication or trace of his lower half. Nothing from the waist on down."

Later, Gloria and her friend compared notes. They found that their descriptions of the man were the same. At this point, Gloria did some further research and discovered that the post hospital— not the morgue, as she had been told—had been at this location.

Gloria's husband, Jim, says, "When I'd go into that nursing home, I'd always have shivering, hair-tingling feelings. I always sensed that there was a presence there."

In recent years, a number of apartments were built close to the old fort—in fact, they were incorporated into the fort itself—and some strange things went on. "A friend of ours," says Jim Watson, "told us that when her boyfriend lived in one of those flats, he would always be aware of cold spots—even on warm days. His friends over there felt the same way. Sometimes, they would say, you could feel a cold spot behind you, as though someone (or some*thing*) was following along behind you!"

This same fellow had other stories. For example, he and other residents of the apartments kept hearing a voice inside the building. It sounded like the name Seth whispered over and over. Even more eerie, says Jim, the men would hear the same name repeated outdoors in a more alarming manner! It was a woman's voice, frantically yelling, "Seth! Seth!" The cries would be repeated continuously and would cover the entire north end of the island, mostly at night and always near the beach.

Are there discarnate entities on Tybee Island? It would seem so. At this unique spot, a tremendous array of people have passed in review over the years. Just think of all the soldiers who arrived, lived here, and departed. In addition to troops who occupied Fort Screven during three wars, there were military personnel here long before then as well. Indeed, there were soldiers in the Savannah area as far back as the very founding of the colony of Georgia in the 1700s.

24

The Ghost in the Old Strachan House

Brunswick

Al Holland reached the landing on his way downstairs. Just a little further and he would have a shocking experience he would never forget.

Now he could almost see the downstairs rooms. He descended a few more steps and something came into view. A human figure stood in the center of the living room. He was a tall man, handsome and dignified. Al, awestruck, stopped cold on the tenth step and just looked.

The figure, well-dressed in a navy blue jacket, light-colored pants, and a dark tie, was not looking toward the stairs but toward the parlor as if overseeing a party of guests. For perhaps half a minute nothing happened. Then the man in the living room dissolved away.

Al kept looking at the spot where the figure had been. He was not so much frightened as excited—and curious. He knew for sure who the distinguished gentleman was! It had to be Mr. Frank Duncan MacPherson Strachan, who had built the large Victorian house on Union Street in Brunswick around 1902. Strachan (pronounced *strawn)* died in the house on Christmas Day in 1931 at the age of sixty.

Al had a strange feeling of peace, of reassurance. After all, this was Strachan's domain, and he was known to have been a kindly, public-spirited businessman. He would certainly not be a malevolent ghost, rather a helpful one—a spirit that would watch over the family.

Al, still musing about his unbidden visitor, walked slowly through the spacious downstairs. As always, he had a feeling of pride and a sense of heritage about the old house, exemplified by the majestic floor plan, along with the furniture and special touches he and his wife, Susan, had added. It must have been like this, he told himself, when under the care of the original owner.

The Scottish Strachans had started a shipping business in 1886, when Frank was just a teenager. Frank's father was a prime mover in the business and was instrumental in developing what soon became a dynasty. The company's volume of trade was especially big in the Far East, where Strachan shipping activity is said to have helped develop the port of Hong Kong.

As a young man, Frank started at the company's Savannah offices, but his entrepreneurial spirit compelled him to move to

Brunswick to start a branch enterprise of his own. Along with others in his family, he had the "golden touch," and his Strachan Line in Brunswick prospered, operating between Brunswick and many world ports.

Sometimes referred to as F.D.M., Frank was known as Brunswick's only millionaire, and he was a millionaire even before coming to the city. More than just a successful businessman, he was a community leader. He played a major role in the development of the St. Simons Island village.

When Al and Susan bought their Union Street house in 1997, it was long after the Strachan family lived there. The house had been sold to outside owners around World War II and had been occupied by several owners since then. Frank had also bought beach property in the early 1900s. It was here that he mounted three cannons facing the sea. The guns, holdovers from the Spanish-American War, were eye-catchers for years, and the story goes that Frank installed them to guard the island from possible invasion by hostile Cubans. A sumptuous home, a famous landmark for years known as the Strachan Cottage, was built on this property during the 1920s. The elegant mansion stood in what was called the King City subdivision, near the village.

One story often told about Frank Strachan was that he had hoped to join the Jekyll Island Club. However, he was refused membership because, according to Al Holland, his family was *nouveau riche*. Club members wanted only those who came from "old money." It's uncertain whether this story is true, but what is certain is that Strachan was disappointed by the refusal.

He was so upset, in fact, that he showed his bitterness by turning on all the lights at his beach house each night at the cocktail hour, making sure the glow could be seen at Jekyll Island. This was his reminder that he was there. He also would fire one of his cannons, they say, just to be sure his presence was observed and noted.

After the death of his father in 1931, F.D.M. Strachan Jr. (also known as Frank) moved with his family into the beach home. It was he who developed special programs of entertainment (games, fireworks, lawn parties, etc.), and his hospitality made the place a landmark for fun and recreation. The good times are remembered with nostalgia by many local citizens.

But these guests at the beach house were not the only visitors! Frank Jr. saw his father here several times after he had passed away. The appearances of the old shipping tycoon were brief. He was seen in various parts of the house—sometimes a misty apparition and sometimes more solid—usually smiling and perhaps wearing his yachting cap. He seemed to be approving of the way his son was maintaining the cottage and providing generous entertainment for the locals.

Visits from Frank Sr. were not limited to the beach house, however. They became international in scope. Frank Jr. used to describe how his dad materialized and talked to him in London.

The shipping business was very successful and the family traveled widely. They stayed at the best hotels, often visiting London, where the company had an office. Even with his prosperity, there were times when Frank Jr. had business worries. He confided to certain friends and family members that at these times he would have "visitations" from his deceased father. During the night in his hotel room, Frank Jr. would hear a sudden "Hello" and there, standing by his bed, would be the familiar figure of Frank Sr. The spirit would begin to talk, telling his son how to handle certain business developments. Sometimes the friendly ghost would sit on the bed for long, serious talks, always on business subjects.

One can only speculate about what the wandering spirit of Frank Sr. thought about the destiny of his fabulous beach house on St. Simons. Undoubtedly, the old lord of the manor was greatly upset. After Frank Jr. died in 1966, the house went through several owners until finally, in the mid-1980s, it was acquired by businesspeople who were developing Daufuskie Island (on the coast of South Carolina). The cottage was floated up to Daufuskie by barge in 1986, where it became the guest house of the Haig Point Resort.

After Al and Susan Holland became owners of the large brick home in Brunswick in the 1990s, they too received visits from Frank Sr. After all, he wanted to be sure the place was properly cared for.

One day, Al was outdoors doing yard work when he looked up and saw a man looking out a first floor window at him. It was Strachan, dressed as before in the dark blue jacket and tie. Once again, his face was clean-shaven and he had no hat. The figure last-

Frank Duncan MacPherson Strachan
(painting courtesy of Al Holland)

ed only briefly and was gone.

Another time the Hollands had a special guest, an attractive young woman who was given the upstairs bedroom that had belonged to Frank Sr. and was where he died. She had some scary moments, too, as she told the Hollands afterwards. Although she never did see anything, she had the uncanny sense that someone was in the room with her. At one point, she was sure someone was sitting on the bed beside her!

Does Frank Strachan still stand guard over his Union Street home? It would appear so, although he is seen only rarely. There is one interesting reminder of him—a painting on the wall in the front hall. His granddaughter, Mrs. William Blum of Savannah, reports that it was painted at the time his sailing yacht *Harpoon* won the first-place trophy in the New York Yacht Club races in 1923. In this portrait, Strachan wears a dark moustache and a dashing yachting cap. He holds a pair of field glasses, and Al comments that the artist might have painted in those field glasses to replace the glass of Scotch whiskey that was usually there!

Al and Susan are sure they have a benevolent spirit watching over their home. They have no fear of this gentle guardian. After all, he is watching over what was once his property.

25

The Spirits of the Timucua Indians

Brighton Island

T he two Indians, a man and a woman, had a look of incredible sadness. They came to John Turner in what seemed to be silent pleading, spreading their hands as if to say, "We need your help."

The shadowy, indistinct forms approached to within three or four feet of John. He saw them in outline only, like the figures in a film negative. They were naked except for breech clouts about their middles. From what he could make out of their faces, John knew they were in the midst of grief. Not a word was spoken, but the message they conveyed was unmistakable.

Previously, John had watched them at a distance as they looked endlessly at the ground as if searching for something. John had the feeling it was something very valuable—perhaps a child?—lost in the swamps or among the palmettos. John could do nothing to help, so the couple finally stopped their silent entreaties and wandered away, still searching for the precious thing they had lost.

This wasn't the only time John had seen apparitions of Native Americans, but it was his closest experience. Exploring alone on Brighton Island near St. Marys in Camden County, he knew the bluff he was standing on was the site of an old Timucua village. At this very spot, John repeatedly saw the vague, darkened forms of Indians. Besides the grief-stricken couple, John also saw a young Timucua girl at a distance. He would observe her, standing motionless in the same spot, on different occasions. Another time, he made out what seemed to be a hunting party, a group of ten or twelve men. They seemed to be carrying weapons—bows and arrows, perhaps, and spears—but John could not make them out clearly.

As a lad, John hunted and fished along the streams and rivers of Brighton Island, and one of his favorite spots was this high bluff overlooking the Crooked River. There were many shells strewn about, remains of Indian garbage dumps, called middens. This spot was the place where the old village stood. Of course, there is nothing left of the village, since the Indians' crude dwellings were made of logs and tree branches, covered with moss and palmetto fronds to keep out the rain. But from this vantage point you can look out over the marshlands, seeing other hammock islands and, in the distance to the east, Cumberland Island.

The Timucua lived as far north as Jekyll Island and as far south as the lower stretches of the St. Johns. Research shows that one of their chiefdoms was Yufera, just to the west of Cumberland Island. The Timucua survived most of the period of European colonization and were even organized into missions by the Spanish, finally succumbing to disease and the onward march of white settlers.

They were noble aborigines, with a high form of culture, being the only native people of Florida and southeast Georgia whose language survives enough to permit significant study. They were dressed only in a crude "body wrap" around the middle and were often tattooed in bizarre patterns. One researcher claims the men wore their hair very long and tucked up neatly around their head. This piling up of the hair served them as a quiver for their arrows when they went to war.

With his love of history and a family lineage that goes back to Revolutionary times, John is proud to have had contact with these ancient people, and he knows that the dwellers of this old Indian village are still there.

John, a retired building contractor, can tell you plenty about kinfolk in southeast Georgia who were soldiers, planters, merchants, and community leaders. He can also tell you some "shivering stories" about the land of his boyhood. Take, for example, his great-great-grandparents, George and Sarah May Turner. George, son of a Revolutionary soldier, and his bride, Sarah May, had twelve children, ten girls and two boys. They lived at Beauvoir, the historic family plantation home near Kingsland. Talk about distinguished ancestry: George was descended from Mary, Queen of Scots, and

Sarah could trace her lineage to Captain James Cook of British naval fame.

Aside from their ancestry, however, the two had more than a normal share of psychic awareness. George, a pioneer white settler and community leader, was thought to be a "skin-walker" by local African Americans. A skin-walker has mystical powers and travels only at night. He has the ability to wear another person's skin and is capable of amazing deeds, both good and evil, then transforming into a vapor. Sarah, on the other hand, was a healer, widely known for rendering cures for a variety of ailments, and she maintained a large supply of healing remedies.

Several years after George and Sarah passed away, their only surviving son, Edward Turner, inherited the family estate of Beauvoir. Edward and his wife, Molly, had an eerie experience every time they walked out the door of their plantation home. Imagine the couple's shock when they looked up and saw, sitting on a branch of a huge oak tree, none other than Sarah herself. She sat neatly on the thick branch, motionless, staring forward, dressed in a long white dress. But the most amazing thing about this spectral tree figure was that at night she became shining and luminous, with a mysterious whitish glow! After a time, Sarah's ghost became a rather common sight. She finally faded away in 1893 and was seen no more.

John, perhaps due to his lineage of ancestors such as these, knows he has the power of ESP or psychic forewarning. In the past, he has been disturbed, even sick, just before family tragedies or

emergencies—and even national calamities. Just before the terrorist attack on September 11, 2001, he was sick for a few days, but this ended on the day of the tragedy.

John has plenty of memories of family members, notable ancestors, and, not to be overlooked, the ancient residents of Camden County! He knows firsthand that this area of southeast Georgia is not only a land of scenic beauty, but a place with hidden wonders in the realm of the supernatural.

26

The Legend of Ebo Landing

St. Simons Island

The woman was alone in her car, driving along Frederica Road on St. Simons Island. It was a windy night, and there was a bright moon overhead. Suddenly, something caught her attention. Looking sideways, she saw a group of four or six men at the side of the road. Although indistinct, they appeared to be bare-chested and barefoot, and their clothes were ragged and hardly enough to cover their bodies. It was too dark to make out their features or the color of their skin.

But the woman could not fail to notice that the men were walking in pairs, shackled together—the right wrist and ankle of one to the left wrist and ankle of another. In a moment, their images dissolved and were gone.

The shackled men, spirits of the night, appeared at this spot for a very good reason. Nearby is a marshy, remote spot known as

Dunbar Creek, close to the western edge of the island. The captives, chained and marching in bondage, were the ghosts of slaves who died at this place long ago. It's the home of "ha'nts," people say, and the tale they tell is a chilling reminder of the cruel days of slavery.

The legend, handed down for generations, centers around one incident in the early 1800s, when plantations here all raised Sea Island cotton, which brought fame and fortune to the Georgia coast. A slave ship loaded with blacks captured in Africa sailed up Dunbar Creek to the place now called Ebo Landing. (This is the name that has persisted through the years, although the spelling of the name has been Americanized and, more accurately, should be "Ibo," or "Igbo.")

According to the old story, the Africans chose suicide over slavery. After turning against their white captors in a mutiny, they marched off the ship and into the water, singing, "The water brought us here and the water will take us away" in their native language.

Well, that's the way the legend goes. However, a close examination of the facts brings out a different story. During the 1980s, Hal Sieber, a North Carolina lecturer and writer, made a study of this subject and delivered a lecture before the Coastal Georgia Historical Society on St. Simons. He titled his oration "The Igbo Stroke: The Factual Basis of the Ebo Landing Legend."

Sieber interviewed descendants of slaves both from the John Couper plantation (at Cannon's Point on the north end of St.

Simons) and the Thomas Spalding plantation on Sapelo Island. Sieber had suspected and was eventually convinced that there had been survivors of the suicide drowning. It wasn't likely that the tale would have been passed on if all of the men had drowned.

Sieber checked with several museums in Georgia and soon learned that a key document containing vital evidence) was in the Philadelphia Museum. It was a letter from the slave dealer who had sold the slaves to Couper and Spalding. Sieber went to Philadelphia and located the letter. He learned that the white overseer and some of the white crewmen had drowned along with the slaves. He also learned how many of the slaves had survived the mutiny. Sieber decided that, since he now had verifiable information, he would go to Africa and continue his research. He knew the Igbo warriors (as they should be properly called) were citizens of the southeastern part of what is now Nigeria. Arriving there, he began interviewing a number of Africans (sometimes with an interpreter), and his results were quite satisfying.

His path took him along the Niger River, south of Benin. Here, while talking to an old man, he mentioned the native chant: "The water brought us and the water will take us away." The old fellow said, "Oh, I know that song," and added that the chant, still sung by boat people along the Niger, was a prayer for everlasting protection to their god, Chukwu, and to the Water Spirit. But the words were actually, "The Water *Spirit* brought us and the Water *Spirit* will take us home." In the native tongue of the Igbos it goes like this:

Orimiri Omambela bu anyi bia,

Orimiri Omambela ka anyi go ejina.

Sieber also learned that a group of Igbos, along with some Angolans also destined for slavery, had been seized in late 1802 by a notorious "slave capture" clan. Through arrangements made by a broker at Calibar, they were delivered to a waiting ship, the *York*, which brought them to Skidaway Island, just southeast of Savannah. Here, a slave importer named Mein prepared about seventy-five of them for shipment to two well-known coastal planters. Thomas Sapulding and John Couper paid about $500 each for the slaves. Ironically, five years earlier, these two men, prominent in Georgia coastal history, had both signed the Georgia Statehood Constitution, which clearly outlawed the importation of Africans.

The *York* brought the captives to Skidaway Island, where they were kept in a holding pen. From Skidaway, the Igbos were transported in mid-May 1803 to Dunbar Creek on St. Simons Island. But the captives revolted before they could be landed, and in the scuffle, Couper's overseer and two crew members leaped overboard and were drowned in vain attempts to reach shore. It was at this point that the Igbo, under the direction of their leader, marched in unison into the creek. At least ten of them died, chanting their prayer for everlasting protection.

Survivors of the melee were taken to Sapelo and Cannon's Point. While in slavery at these locations, they passed on their recollections to their children and relatives. Through descendants, the eyewitness accounts of these survivors became the legend of Ebo Landing. All of this background information, along with the detailed account by the slave importer who sold the Igbos, has verified the legend's historical content.

But perhaps most interesting of all is the ghost story! Ever since the tragic event, you can hear chanting, moaning, and the rattling of chains near the bluff adjacent to the sewage treatment plant at Dunbar Creek. To this day, there are those who avoid Ebo Landing after dark. "Don't go down there," they say. "It's haunted."

Harry Paisley conducts ghost tours for Misty Oaks Carriage Tours. Starting at the St. Simons village, he leads groups of tourists on a rambling walk to various points of interest, including haunted spots. One of his tour customers told him an eerie tale. This woman, who lived in a large residential area close to Dunbar Creek, happened to wake up in the middle of the night. At the foot of the bed stood an indistinct human form. He appeared wild-looking, somewhat fierce and grim, and stayed only a moment before he disappeared.

Are the ghostly sightings by this woman and the woman in her car related to what happened at Ebo Landing so many years ago? Harry Paisley thinks so.

Research shows that of the many African tribes sold into slavery, the Igbos were known to have been fiercely independent. It is entirely logical that they would have rebelled against their captors, drowning themselves as an alternative to a lifetime of servitude.

27

The Spirit
That Lingered

Camden County

What sort of unseen spirit was it that wouldn't leave that home in Camden County? It was a simple, one-story frame house in the Kingsland area. Built in 1957, the place seemed comfortable to Jack and Mary Crandon when they bought it in 1997, but it needed work. Jack, a handyman, went about fixing and even remodeling. One of his projects was to change the layout of the rooms, realigning walls and covering up and adding doors in certain places. Jack didn't realize that the changes he was making were going to confuse and agitate a certain other "occupant" of the house, an occupant who wasn't going to remain quiet about it. Soon after they moved in, Jack and Mary began to suspect that they were sharing their abode with a "something else" nobody could see—not necessarily an evil entity, but one with definite opinions about how things should be!

143

There were noises. A *klunk-klunk* would be heard, sometimes followed by the sound of furniture or boxes being dragged across the floor or something falling off a table. Hearing the noises at night, Jack would get up to investigate, always with the same results: nothing there. Also, objects would be moved by an unseen hand! An item left on a table would be found later in the kitchen or a bedroom. Neither Jack, Mary, nor teenaged son Ronnie had moved the item, but someone did.

Then came an unforgettable happening. One night while Mary and Ronnie were sitting in the living room, they heard heavy footsteps crossing the floor. Something forged a path diagonally across the room from the front door to the bedroom door. "Did you hear that?" asked Mary, trying to be brave as she forced a smile. They both realized that an entity had just entered the house and made definite tracks across the room.

Jack and Mary had bought the house from Jake Martin, a nearby resident who was also a friend. Martin lived there prior to the Crandons; in fact, it was his old family home. At this point, Mary decided to investigate.

"I think we have a ghost," she told Jake.

"Yes," said Jake. "That's my father, Clarence. He died in the house and is still there. I'm sure of it. We used to hear him moving around after he passed away."

This didn't bother Mary an awful lot because Clarence was described as a short, mild-mannered man who "never harmed anybody." She talked it over with Jack. The two of them decided that, even thought they didn't like the situation, they would go ahead and live with the ghost, hoping he wouldn't bother them too much or turn violent.

But from that point on, the ghost seemed to be a lot more active. The noises continued, mostly in the living room at night but sometimes in other parts of the house. Strange noises and *klunks* came from Ronnie's room. And objects kept disappearing too.

Jack was a self-employed auto repairman, and people would bring their cars to his house to have them fixed. On one occasion, Jack sweated over a tough job—an older model in bad shape—but couldn't fix it. He told the owner to come and pick it up. Somewhat irritated, the owner showed up.

"Where are my keys?" he asked.

Jack, knowing where he'd left them, ran into the house and opened the top bureau drawer. No keys. This made the owner even madder, but there was no way Jack could explain the ghost. "We'll just keep looking around the house," he said.

Jack took the seething fellow home, apologizing all the way. For the next several days, the man called again and again, bugging the Crandons for his keys. They looked for three weeks before Jack finally found them—right in the top drawer where he had left them!

Another story involves two christening outfits, belonging to Mary and her brother, packed in separate cedar chests. These were nicely pressed and clean, ready to be worn for the upcoming baptism of a relative. What could Clarence have possibly wanted with such items? Why would he move them? One day, Mary and Jack discovered that Mary's brother's outfit had disappeared completely (they never did find it), and Mary's was missing from its cedar chest, then later found, dumped crudely on a closet floor.

There were mysteries in the kitchen too, such as the missing box of floor tile. When Jack was almost done retiling the floor (only a single strip to do), the whole box disappeared. "Guess the old boy didn't like our pattern," Jack and Mary concluded.

Another time Jack wanted to make chili dogs, so he was heating chili in a sauce pan. He left the kitchen for a moment and when he returned, the burner switch was turned off and the pan had been slid halfway off the burner.

Jake Martin remembered only one sighting of the ghost when he lived in the house, but his brother saw an apparition many times. In fact, when Jake awoke, it was common for his brother to tell him, "I had another glimpse of a man during the night. He looked like Dad. Then he disappeared."

Mary also had a sighting—if it can be called that. She was waking up one morning and saw a misty, shapeless mass, almost smoky in appearance. It was in one corner of the room. Mary, still not quite awake, did not "register" for a moment. But this brief vision of something that didn't belong there gave her the creeps, so she pulled the covers up over her head!

"Good bye," she yelled. There was nothing visible later when she peeked out.

Jack and Mary reported in the latter part of 1999 that Clarence Martin's widow had died—and suddenly the ghost stopped all his activities. Since then, things have been quiet in the Crandon household. Jack and Mary are glad, in a way, that everything is peaceful, but they're also sad to think that the ghost is no longer "doing his thing."

Is Clarence Martin gone for good? Alas, no one knows.

Epilogue

This book began with one of those why-doesn't-somebody complaints. I was leaving a bookstore on Jekyll Island when the owner turned to me and said someone needed to write a book about the ghosts of the coastal islands.

"Just think of all the history along here," he said. "There must be millions of old spirits and phantoms in this area!"

Well, one thing led to another and I accepted the challenge. I had always had an interest in ghosts and, while living in the Midwest, had even written a self-published book on the subject. I thought it would be an interesting project.

That was about six years ago. I began collecting information, setting up interviews, and taking notes, but then I got hopelessly sidetracked with other activities. I was doing freelance business articles, writing a column for a weekly paper, and spending time in community activities. I decided to put the ghost writing on hold for a while.

I'm glad I saved my notes. Around 1998 I plunged back into it, equipped with some new stories from reliable witnesses. I soon had many chapters assembled that seemed to go together well. But every so often I would pause in my work and ask myself, Is there really something out there?

The question is a reasonable one. Skeptics have always been

with us, and there are frequent scientific put-downs and negative views on the subject of ghosts. Skeptics can be amusing. The late Bergen Evans (wit, author, and Northwestern University professor) devoted a book to a caustic pooh-pooh of the supernatural. He called it *The Spoor of Spooks,* and it is full of lines like this: "Ghosts are good for half a column any day the criminals are resting."

Evans told how in 1953 *Life* magazine obtained for its readers what was supposed to be an actual photo of the spirit of France's Unknown Soldier. *Life* had a close-up of a white, eerie face that the editors insisted had slowly formed in the flame that burns over the Unknown Soldier's grave under the Arc de Triomphe in Paris. Evans wrote: "The close-up view, which the editors supplied, showed something resembling a baboon's skull and raised conjecture as to whether a patriotic simian had not slipped by a lenient draft board." If you're a serious investigator of the occult, such accounts will merely amuse you as you go on in your quest for a greater dimension of understanding.

I am often asked if I am a believer. The answer is yes, although I have never had an encounter with a ghost. I tell people that my understanding is weak but that I know there surely are happenings we don't understand. It also seems that one must have a certain psychic awareness, the right sort of R and R (relaxed and receptive) mind for an encounter to take place. You must be relaxed, not looking intensely for an entity, and also mentally receptive to the occult signals being transmitted.

Although some of these accounts are old legends that have been around for generations, most were recently related to me personally. All are presented from the viewpoint of an investigator who does not claim to be a medium or spiritualist. I merely collected the details and set it all down on paper. In almost every case, names were changed to ensure privacy. Locations of the haunted places were identified only in general terms to protect them and the people who live near them.

And so I bid you farewell with the reminder that there are fascinating and mysterious things going on, and I think they deserve our attention, our respect, and our interest. We should continue to be mighty curious and to ask questions! And whatever you find out, I hope you will share it with me. Write to me in care of the publisher.

If you enjoyed reading this book, here are some other books from Pineapple Press on related topics. For a complete catalog, write to Pineapple Press, P.O. Box 3889, Sarasota, FL 34230 or call 1-800-PINEAPL (746-3275). Or visit our website at www.pineapplepress.com.

Bansemer's Book of Carolina and Georgia Lighthouses by Roger Bansemer. Roger Bansemer's beautiful paintings accurately portray how each lighthouse along the coasts of the Carolinas and Georgia looks today. ISBN 1-56164-194-4 (hb)

The Best Ghost Tales of North Carolina by Terrance Zepke. The actors of North Carolina's past linger among the living in this thrilling collection of ghost tales. ISBN 1-56164-233-9 (pb)

Exploring South Carolina's Islands by Terrance Zepke. A complete guide for vacationers, day-trippers, and armchair travelers. ISBN 1-56164-259-2 (pb)

Georgia's Lighthouses and Historic Coastal Sites by Kevin M. McCarthy. With full-color paintings by maritime artist William L. Trotter, this book traces the history of 30 sites. ISBN 1-56164-143-X (pb)

Ghosts of the Carolina Coasts by Terrance Zepke. Taken from real-life occurrences and Carolina Lowcountry lore, these 32 spine-tingling ghost stories take place in prominent historic structures of the region. ISBN 1-56164-175-8 (pb)

Ghosts of St. Augustine by Dave Lapham. The unique and often turbulent history of America's oldest city is told in 24 spooky stories that cover 400 years' worth of ghosts. ISBN 1-56164-123-5 (pb)

Haunt Hunter's Guide to Florida by Joyce Elson Moore. Visit 37 haunted sites, each with its "haunt history," interviews, directions, and travel tips. ISBN 1-56164-150-2 (pb)

Haunting Sunshine by Jack Powell. Explore the darker side of the Sunshine State. Tour Florida's places and history through some of its best ghost stories. ISBN 1-56164-220-7 (pb)

Oldest Ghosts by Karen Harvey. Read about more St. Augustine ghosts. Includes interviews with people who share their homes with restless spirits. ISBN 1-56164-222-3 (pb)